D0519921

CHRISTMAS IN MY HEART®

24

JOE L. WHEELER

"For lo, the Holy Child is born—
And holy is the night."
— Parmenter (8)

[signature]

Conifer, Colorado
10 - 30 - 15

Pacific Press®
Publishing Association
Nampa, Idaho | Oshawa, Ontario, Canada
www.pacificpress.com

Copyright © 2015 by Joe L. Wheeler
Printed in the United States of America
All rights reserved

Cover design by Steve Lanto
Cover art by George Henry Durrie
Interior illustrations from the library of Joe L. Wheeler
Interior design by Kristin Hansen-Mellish

The author assumes full responsibility for the accuracy of all facts and
quotations as cited in this book.

Christmas in My Heart® is a registered trademark of Joe L. Wheeler and
may not be used by anyone else in any form. Visit Joe Wheeler's Web site at
www.joewheelerbooks.com. Representing the author is WordServe Literary
Group, Ltd., 7061 S. University Blvd., Suite 307, Centennial, CO 80122.

Additional copies of this book are available by calling toll-free
1-800-765-6955 or by visiting www.adventistbookcenter.com.

Scripture quotations marked NLT are taken from the Holy Bible, New
Living Translation, copyright © 1996. Used by permission of Tyndale House
Publishers, Inc., Wheaton, Illinois 60189. All rights reserved.

None of these stories may be reprinted or placed on the Internet without
the express written permission of the editor/compiler, Joe L. Wheeler (P.O.
Box 1246, Conifer, CO 80433), or the copyright holder.

Library of Congress Cataloging-in-Publication Data:

Wheeler, Joe L., 1936–   comp.
  Christmas in my heart. Book 24.
  1. Christmas stories, American. I. Title:
Christmas in my heart. Book 24.

ISBN 13: 978-0-8163-5780-2
ISBN 10: 0-8163-5780-3

August 2015

Dedication

Through the years, no one has loved the Christmas in My Heart® stories more than she has. In fact, she cherishes our story collections so much that she has tabulated *every story* and *every author* so that readers can more easily access specific stories or authors they are searching for. And every year that passes, she adds all the recent story data to the existing lists—a monumental task, given the number of stories in our now seventy-six story anthologies. Thus, it gives me great joy to dedicate *Christmas in My Heart 24* to

ELLEN FRANCISCO
of
Ooltewah, Tennessee.

Books by Joe L. Wheeler

Acknowledgments

Frontispiece poem, "Holy Night," by Catherine Parmenter. Published in *St. Nicholas*, December 1937. Original text owned by Joe Wheeler.

Introduction: "Our Top Twenty Christmas Stories," by Joseph Leininger Wheeler. Copyright © 2014. Printed by permission of the author. All rights reserved.

"A Wood Crowns the Waters," by Eric Philbrook Kelly. Published in *St. Nicholas*, December 1934. Original text owned by Joe Wheeler.

"Little Cherry's Star," by G. M. Farley. Published in Farley's book *Little Cherry's Star and Other Stories* (private printing, 1965). Used by permission of the author.

"The Christmas Kink," by Lucille Adams. Published in *Sunshine Magazine*, December 1956. Reprinted by permission of Garth Hendrichs and *Sunshine Magazine*.

"Flight Before Christmas," by John Scott Douglas. Published in *Young People's Weekly*, December 6, 1936. Printed by permission of Joe Wheeler (P.O. Box 1246, Conifer, CO 80433) and David C. Cook (4050 Lee Vance View, Colorado Springs, CO 80918).

"Denny's Christmas Revelation," by Faith Freeborn Turner. Published in a tract printed by Pilgrim Tract Society, Randlemann, NC. Reprinted by permission of Pilgrim Tract Society, Inc.

"The Belated Christmas Train," by William McGinnies. Published in *Ladies' Home Journal*, December 1904. Original text owned by Joe Wheeler.

"Joy to the World," by Mary Russell. Published in *Young People's Weekly*, Dec. 19, 1937. Printed by permission of Joe Wheeler (P.O. Box 1246, Conifer, CO 80433) and David C. Cook (4050 Lee Vance View, Colorado Springs, CO 80918).

"The Lighted Path," by Temple Bailey. Published in Bailey's book *So This Is Christmas! and Other Christmas Stories* (Philadelphia: Penn Pub., 1931). Original text owned by Joe Wheeler.

"Let Nothing You Dismay," by Ruth P. Harnden. Published in *Collier's Weekly*, December 23, 1950. If anyone knows the whereabouts of the author or the author's next of kin of this story, please contact Joe Wheeler (P.O. Box 1246, Conifer, CO 80433).

"A Warmth in Her Heart," by Goldie Down. Published in *Signs of the Times*, December 1983. Printed by permission of *Signs of the Times.* If anyone knows the whereabouts of the author of this story, please contact Joe Wheeler (P.O. Box 1246, Conifer, CO 80433).

"The Lost Child," as retold by Mabel Lee Cooper. Published in *The Girls' Companion,* December 18 and 25, 1938. Printed by permission of Joe Wheeler (P.O. Box 1246, Conifer, CO 80433) and David C. Cook (4050 Lee Vance View, Colorado Springs, CO 80918).

"Celestial Roots," by Thomas Vallance. Published in *Sunshine Magazine,* December 1959. Reprinted by permission of Garth Henrichs and *Sunshine Magazine.*

"A Story for Christmas," by Jody Shields. Published in *The Relief Society Magazine,* December 1968. If anyone knows the whereabouts of the author or of the author's next of kin, please contact Joe Wheeler (P.O. Box 1246, Conifer, CO 80433).

"The Baby Camel That Walked to Jesus," by Walter A. Dyer. Published in *Ladies' Home Journal,* Christmas 1914. Original text owned by Joe Wheeler.

"Choices," by Isobel Stewart. Published in *The People's Friend,* Christmas 2006. Reprinted by permission of Derek Stewart.

"The Dream Catcher," by Joseph Leininger Wheeler. Copyright © 2014. Printed by permission of the author. All rights reserved.

* * * * *

Contents

Holy Night

Catherine Parmenter

On all things ugly and forlorn
Beauty now is laid . . .
This night the Lord of life is born
To a gentle maid.

And down the silent roads of earth
Angels singing move,
Whose praises bless His humble birth—
Little Lord of love!

The darkness is no longer dark:
Proud the star of heaven
That flames across the sky to mark
Him whom God hath given.

To all things ugly and forlorn—
Beauty, song and light!
For lo, the Holy Child is born—
And holy is the night!

Our Top Twenty Christmas Stories

Joseph Leininger Wheeler

For two years now, I have been taking a survey, polling only those very special people who admit to being "completists." In other words, they have *all* the *Christmas in My Heart*® books. But even though there are thousands who do, I have discovered that it is extremely difficult to get anyone to take the time to reread all 374 Christmas stories (includes three stories that were in the Focus on the Family/Tyndale House *Christmas in My Heart 13* and *Christmas in My Heart 15* hardbacks, but are not in the core Currier & Ives series). To then actually rank the ones perceived as the "greatest" is not a task for the faint of heart!

Respondents are unanimous in declaring they find it all but impossible to arrive at definitive ranked lists. Nevertheless, many have tried. Thanks to them, we've come up with this list. Keep in mind that we are counting only Christmas stories that actually appeared in our own series. In our balloting, few stories garnered more than four or five votes. You'll note that our base is eight votes. The rankings are also based on the highest to lowest rankings within a given vote category.

I felt it would be incredibly presumptuous for me to vote, since I've written a number of these stories myself. Nevertheless, you'll note that I have included a list of my favorite stories too.

Top twenty	Votes
1. "Pandora's Books," by Joe L. Wheeler	21
2. " 'Meditation' in a Minor Key," by Joe L. Wheeler	17
3. "The Tiny Foot," by Frederic Loomis	20
4. "The Gold and Ivory Tablecloth," by Howard C. Schade	18
5. "Evensong," by Joe L. Wheeler	14
6. "The Best Christmas Pageant Ever," by Barbara Robinson	13
7. "The Littlest Orphan and the Christ Baby," by Margaret E. Sangster	12
8. "How an Unborn Baby Saved Its Mother's Life," by MacDougall and How	12
9. "Christmas Day in the Morning," by Pearl Buck	12
10. "Truce in the Forest," by Fritz Vincken	11
11. "A Few Bars in the Key of G," by Clifton Carlisle Osborne	11
12. "Johnny Christmas," Author Unknown	11
13. "David's Star of Bethlehem," by Christine Whiting Parmenter	10
14. "The Third Rose," by Joe L. Wheeler	10
15. "Small Things," by Margaret E. Sangster	10
16. "The Red Mittens," by Hartley F. Dailey	9
17. "At Lowest Ebb," Author Unknown	8
18. "Roses in December," by Sybil Haddock	8
19. "A Rose in Winter," by Jodi Detrick	8
20. "The Missionary Barrel," by Carolyn Abbott Stanley	8

And now for my own. It's unlikely that any of you will agree 100 percent with my rankings either.

Wheeler's top twenty

1. "The Story of the Other Wise Man," by Henry Van Dyke
2. "A Few Bars in the Key of G," by Clifton Carlisle Osborne
3. "The Littlest Orphan and the Christ Baby," by Margaret E. Sangster
4. "David's Star of Bethlehem," by Christine Whiting Parmenter
5. "The Tiny Foot," by Frederick Loomis
6. "The Gold and Ivory Tablecloth," by Howard C. Schade
7. "Merry Little Christmas," by Agnes Sligh Turnbull
8. "Christmas Day in the Morning," by Pearl Buck
9. "The Best Christmas Pageant Ever," by Barbara Robinson
10. "Truce in the Forest," by Fritz Vincken
11. "The Last Straw," by Paula McDonald Palangi
12. "A String of Blue Beads," by Fulton Oursler
13. "The Candle in the Forest," by Temple Bailey
14. "And It Was Christmas Morning," by Temple Bailey
15. "Joyful *and* Triumphant," by John McCain
16. "A Certain Small Shepherd," by Rebecca Caudill
17. "Why the Minister Did Not Resign," Author Unknown
18. "The Jubilee Agreement," by Terry Beck
19. "Delayed Delivery," by Cathy Miller
20. "The Red Envelope," by Nancy N. Rue

About this collection

Most of the authors in this collection will be new to our readers, with only three exceptions: this is Eric Philbrook Kelly's fourth appearance in the series, Isobel Stewart's sixth, and Temple Bailey's twelfth.

Coda

I always look forward to hearing from you! Please do keep the stories, responses, and suggestions coming—and not just for Christmas stories. I am putting together collections of other genres as well. You may reach me by writing to:

Joe L. Wheeler, PhD
P.O. Box 1246
Conifer, CO 80433

May the Lord bless and guide the ministry of these stories in your home.

A Wood Crowns the Waters

Eric Philbrook Kelly

On a Christmas Eve long ago and far away, an eight-year-old girl and an old man waited to hear the ringing of the bells in the village far below their homes, which were high in the Carpathian Mountains. War had taken the old man's family, and the anguish he'd experienced had caused him to lose his mind for a time.

When midnight came, the bells rang, and the sound of their ringing was followed by music of a softer sort that only the girl could hear. What in the lonely crags around them was the source of that ethereal music?

* * * * *

In modern history, no European nation has suffered more than Poland. And no Western writer has done more to preserve its story legacy than Eric Philbrook Kelly. This may very well be his greatest Christmas story of all.

* * * * *

Christmas Eve again. The old world had rolled its weary course through another year of work and joy and labor and suffering; a year of failure and success, of tears and smiles, of births and deaths, and now there had come that moment when there was to be an end of all the things that had belonged to the year, for Christ was to be born, and life would commence anew.

High up in the dizzy silences of the Tatry peaks of the Carpathians, the crystal air was still dark blue with early dusk, and the first star that had announced the coming of the Royal Child was still brilliant near the horizon's edge, although many thousands of its bright companions were now twinkling in the depths of the sky.

Perched high upon a huge rock above the path that came from the land beyond the mountains, anciently called Bohemia, were the ruins of an old castle. How long they had been there no man could remember, and in the earliest chronicles of the villages that lay either side of the range they were referred to as ruins. The crumbling stage of them had long since passed away; the four flanking roofless towers, the round donjon in the center, the walls of the palace, and the buttressed supports of an ancient chapel had been worn smooth and round by time and weather. Men built much better in the old days than at the present, and these monuments of antiquity were designed to last until the Day of Judgment. It is probable that they would have stood as originally built had not the destroying hand of man defaced them. War after war had swept across these mountains from the earliest days when Goth or Magyar or Hun besieged this keep, though it was probably in the days of Genghis Khan or Batu that the castle had been pillaged and burned.

Amidst the ruins of the castle on this particular Christmas Eve there stood looking down upon the lights of the distant villages an old man and a young girl. The starlight that is always exceptionally brilliant in these mountains threw into visibility the outlines of the peaks above them and the jagged slopes that stretched away down toward Zakopane. At a distance, they could see the stars collected in that mirroring lake, the Eye of the Sea; and the Milky Way was reflected across it like a ribbon of fire. The air, though cold, was not piercing, and the way in which objects seen through it appeared near and large was akin to a miracle. Anusia, the eight-year-old daughter of Goral Jacek, stood beside Old Michal looking out at the splendor of the night, but her mind was less on the mountains than on the villages.

"There are trees in the market and booths with sweets and dolls and toys," she said. "My father will return tomorrow with presents."

"That he will, my child. And we will have our Christmas feast up here. I have *such* a goose."

She clapped her hands. "And will we hear the bells?" she asked.

"I think so. If the air is as it is now, we will hear the midnight bells from Zakopane and perhaps from Nowy Targ."

"Next year I shall be in the village," she said. "And then I shall go to the church and hear the singing and see the Christ Child by the altar. There will be a *szopka* [crèche] and *kolędy* [Nativity hymns]. What happiness it will be!"

"That you will," said the old man. "When I was a boy, I was in Krakow. That's where they celebrate Christmas as nowhere else in the world. Then the great organ is played in the church of Panna Maria, the trumpeters come out in the tower, and a thousand voices carry up the carols to God in the sky."

Saying this, he abruptly led the child into his hut, built against the wall on the side of the ruin that looked down upon the footpath. It was pleasant there despite the roughness and crudity of the construction. There were two rooms in the little structure, the first a living and dining room into which they had come. The walls were double and well papered; there were two windows, curtained; and a table sat in the middle of the room with a lamp upon it and books scattered about. If Old Michal were a hermit, he was at least a book-loving hermit.

Anusia threw off her wool-lined

leather jacket and sat down in one of the chairs and began to look at pictures. She was fair haired, with blue eyes, and dressed in true mountain fashion with a full skirt and laced bodice. The old man, though in the garb of the mountaineer—white skin trousers, leather sleeveless vest, cape and round hat with its circle of small shells—was not broad featured like the mountain folk. He had an ageless face with fine features like those of the landowning class, or *szlachta*.

"Can you stay awake until midnight?" asked the old man.

"I shall stay awake," declared Anusia. "At midnight I shall go out to listen to the bells . . .

"When I was very little they told me that some people can hear music in the sky then. Do you think they can?"

"I have heard no music for many a year," said he sadly. "Yet on this night when Christ is born it must be that angels sing in the sky."

"Will you not listen for this other music when the bells begin?"

"That I shall. Perhaps we will hear them this night. I have listened on many Christmas Eves before this, but either the wind was howling or there was a storm—"

"Father Michal," the girl asked, interrupting him, "have you always lived up here alone? Have you never had a home down in a village or in the city?"

The old man was silent for so long that Anusia thought he hadn't heard her. He was somewhat deaf, was the old man, yet he had a faculty for catching what people said. And Anusia's question was one that arose naturally, since her own mother had died in the little stone house she now occupied with her father down the sloping road that led to Zakopane.

Anusia had been much in the company of Old Michal,

who delighted in her presence. He was nominally a watchman on the grounds of Pan Lubomirski, an extensive grounds that extended clear across the Galician plain into the mountains. But instead of living in the watchman's house down on the plain, he had chosen to make his home here in the ruins of the old castle that bordered the estate. Anusia remembered him from her earliest days. He was always kind and gentle, yet full of strength and vigor. On stormy nights, he was often seen with his lantern and a coil of rope patrolling the path that ran through the mountains. Many a passerby—peasant or herder or strolling peddler—had shaped the difficult course amidst the treacherous cliffs by the light of that lantern, and had found food and comfort in the hut amid the ruins.

There was much speculation about Michal in the village. He had inhabited this place ever since the first years of the Great War. Pan Lubomirski himself had found him wandering in a daze about the mountains the night after the Germans and Austrians had taken their prisoners across this pass. Though the owner of the land couldn't recognize Michal's history, nor could he tell the owner everything clearly since at that time his mind was in a whirl, the owner had given him employment and permission to make his habitation there. In that place he lived, making only occasional trips to the villages for supplies. In time, he had sheep in the folds below the slopes, a garden on the rich Lubomirski meadows, and goats that furnished him with milk and cheese in his lonely dwelling.

For eighteen years, Michal had lived there, and but little of his history was known to the country about. For one thing, there were but few interested, and for another, he was loath—or perhaps unable—to speak of himself. Some thought it was

as if his memory had failed him, either because of age or a shock of some sort. The older folks knew that he had not been there before the war, and the younger, with whom he was ever a favorite, cared little about his past since he was so firmly in the present.

"You ask me if I had another home. Yes, my child, a home and a wife."

Anusia stared at him. There was something in his voice that she had never heard before; yet child though she was, she knew that it was the symbol of some deep feeling and that deep feeling was communicable and affected her strongly.

"Had you a daughter like me?" she asked.

"No," he said, and he smiled down at her. "No daughter. A son is what I had."

"Father Michal, was he as old as I?"

"Much older. He would be as old as your father now."

"But I don't understand. Where is he now?"

Michal went to the stove in the corner and thrust some wood in it. Then, returning, he sat down at the table and looked at Anusia. "My child," he said, and she noticed that tears had come into his eyes, "I do not know. And if I could only know I would be the happiest man on earth."

"But where did he go?"

"Nowhere of his own accord. We had a *dwor* [small country house] in Krasnik in the Lublin District. That was eighteen years ago."

He was silent again, musing, dreaming. He had not spoken this freely in all the years since then. Perhaps he was willing to tell of this sadness because it was Christmas Eve. Perhaps because the love he bore for the neighbor's child touched him powerfully. Perhaps because his mind, which had been numb with suffering under shock for so long, had at length worked itself free.

"When the war broke out in 1914, he was taken to the Russian Army. His company was stationed in our town, and I saw him every day. But then there was fighting. I cannot tell you what it all means, you wouldn't understand. The armies advanced against each other, and the Germans and Austrians captured the company in which my son fought. All day the battle raged over our heads. My home was destroyed, my wife was killed, the land was ruined . . . and then at sundown they led my son away a captive, to take him to a prison in Austria or Germany."

Anusia was afraid to ask him more about this, though she understood little of it except that his son was taken away.

"And did you never hear from him?"

He shook his head. "He died in prison I, think."

"How did you come here, Father Michal?"

"This is the way the soldiers came. He was a prisoner among them, and I followed."

"Did they bring him here through the mountains?"

"Yes. They led him through the pass. I was crazed with the grief of losing my home and my wife already . . . I followed and followed, hoping that I might be near him. At last there came orders that none were to follow the prisoners. They told me to remain behind. I saw my son led away. Then darkness came over me, and when I recovered my senses Pan Lubomirski's servants carried me up to the great house."

"Poor Father Michal," the child said and threw her arms about his neck.

"I was not myself again for many years. (Why he said this to a child who should know nothing of such things, I do not

know.) But I always felt that if my son ever came back to Poland, he would come by this pass. It was here that he saw me last, and I him. In the beginning, it was a certainty in my mind that I should see him, yet as years passed and my mind became stronger I was not so sure."

"Have you ever been back to Krasnik?"

"Never. For many years, I had forgotten whence I came. Then when my brain was clearer, I knew that all had forgotten me. Pan Lubomirski did his best to find my son, but all traces of him in the prison camps was lost, and no letters came. Pan has even sent men to Krasnik. If my son did return there, as I scarce believe, he must have found only desolation. And if letters went there in those days when my mind was feeble, they were returned, no doubt, since I was counted among the dead."

Anusia pondered for several minutes. Then she said, "I think he will come sometime, Father Michal. He will come and find you.

"You know how it is on Christmas Day. When we have our Christmas dinner, we always leave one vacant place at the table. That's for the Christ Child if He should come in. If the Christ Child might come, why might not your son come? I will always think of him on Christmas Day and ask in my prayers that he be sent back to you . . . But this is Christmas Eve, and you must tell me some of the stories you told your boy when you lived in Krasnik."

He was glad to change to the brighter theme, yet the thoughts of his loved ones had washed some bitter silences from his heart, and he not only told the old stories but he also sang some of the old songs, until at length the child laid her head upon her hands at the table, and her eyes, growing heavier and heavier, closed in sleep.

He would let her sleep so until it became midnight, and then he would take her out on the ramparts to hear the village bells, after which she should have the cot in the bedroom while he spent the night on a couch. Then early in the morning Jacek would be back from the village with presents for his daughter, and all three would dine with rejoicing upon the fat goose that hung just outside the door.

* * * * *

But Michal did not go to his books while she slept. Instead, his mind wandered back over the old days when he had lived with his family in Krasnik. How joyous they were in those times! What Christmases they had! How the boys used to go round with a star and a puppet theater and act out scenes from *Szopka Krakowska*. They would sing all the old *kol dy*. How joyous it was when the first star appeared and the angel rang the bell outside and they all rushed out to see the star. They never saw the angel, though. And then the figures in gold and silver upon the candle-hung tree, the presents and the kisses . . . And at the end they would all gather and sing that forbidden *mazurka* of Dombrowski, that song of the Polish legions of Napoleon.

Then grief had come upon them like a thunderbolt. His father and mother had been sent to Siberia. His brother had died in America. Finally, when he himself had married and hoped to live in peace and bring up his son to live at home and cultivate the land, the war had broken out just as the son came home from the university with his degree. Fire and blood, pestilence and famine, and then amidst the

roar of flames and the bursting of shells and the cries of the stricken—then his home had been destroyed, his wife killed, his son led away a captive.

Could the boy be alive? He would be a man of forty by now.

In those first few years, he had told Pan Lubomirski all that he could remember and a search for his son had been made. It was quite evident that the boy had thought him dead, and there could be no other hope save that his boy had not died amidst suffering. No word from abroad nor from the post. It must be that way. But for eighteen years, he had lived in this pass and had scrutinized the face of each passerby in the vain hope that it might be his son returning. In the beginning, the feeling that his son would one day return that way had been strong; but as years passed and his reason was mended, it seemed less and less likely that he would ever see his own again. But as the saying goes, "Time heals all wounds." Now his life was useful, and he was happy in it, and Goral Jacek was very friendly. So, he loved Jacek's daughter, and he lavished upon her the learning that he had received of old when there was a tutor in his own family.

Time sped on, and midnight approached.

"Wake up, Anusia," Michal said as he touched her gently on the shoulder.

She lifted a mass of yellow hair out of which two sleepy eyes glistened.

"In a minute it will be midnight, and there will be bells."

The word *bells* brought her to her feet. "Father Michal, I didn't mean to sleep. It isn't too late?"

"No, child. It is just time."

He adjusted a cape of heavy wool about his jacket while she hooked her fur-lined woolen coat and covered her head with a heavy kerchief. Then they went out into the night.

For a few moments, they were blind to the scene, and then objects and lights began to appear. First, it was the sky alive with stars that they saw, and soon it was the shadow of the peaks against them. Then the valley unrolled slowly and the villages below began to take shape. Zakopane emerged first like a toy village cut in cardboard, the boards furnished with colored papers that created blue and green effects where the light shone through, the windows like slits in the walls, the outside lamps like pinpoints of luminescence. Then Nowy Targ and other villages beyond threw the reflections of their lights into the sky. There was no wind, and the two stood like carven figures against the huge background of rock.

All at once the Christ was born. At that, the great bell on the Zakopane church caught the message and began to sound; then the bells on the town hall and the nearby villages followed. The impulse seemed to pass over their heads like a little breeze, the stars seemed to flare, the old man and the child felt a sudden stirring of heart . . . How many years ago it was that shepherds from hills like these hurried south to Bethlehem to greet the newborn Child. What joy it would be now to seek out One who had come to end the hateful enmities of men and bring peace everlasting.

Yet now—and this they realized with keen happiness— there was no need to go to a foreign country. The Christ Child who brought all good things had come to them. The night air was so clear, so charged with life, that the pealing of the bells came plainly to their ears, though the bells were many miles away. *Clang, clang, clang.*

The child was in an ecstasy of joy. For the moment, she

forgot everything: her companion, her humble home, the great peaks and deep lakes about her. The sound of the bells carried her out into the deep vistas of space that lay about the stars. *Clang, clang, clang.* Everywhere bells were sounding music that was glad, and loud, and sweet.

Then all at once there drifted to her ears another sound. It, too, was music, and although at first it seemed to be a part of the song of the bells, yet it later separated from that and floated through the air by itself. It was faint—so faint as to be hardly perceptible. Yet it was sweet, far sweeter than the peals of joy from those clamorous metal mouths. And it was a song—more than that, she realized with a start—it was a song that she knew!

The spell that encompassed her suddenly broke. She was alive again, and real and in a real world, and the fingers that clasped hers were real and living and loved. In excitement she turned to the old man.

"Father Michal! Father Michal!"

He bent down.

"I hear music."

"It is the bells," he exclaimed. "My hearing is not good, but there is something in this air that makes one hear. I can hear them faintly too."

"But there is other music besides the bells."

"Other music?"

"Did you not say that one could hear other music on Christmas Eve? I have heard it, and I can hear it now."

He listened silently. "I cannot hear."

"But I can. And I know the song. It is the song they sing in the church: 'Through Night's Dark Shadow.' "

"Are you sure, child?"

"Yes, I am sure . . . It is over there," and she pointed in the direction from which the music came.

He faced the direction her finger indicated and asked, "Do you still hear it?"

"Yes. It goes on and on. Could it be an angel's song?"

He was silent. "No, my child," he said at length. "Were that so I might hear it as well. This is no heavenly music. It is some human being. And in the direction in which you point there are steep cliffs that fall clear to the valley. I must go there and see who it is. It would be dangerous for anyone who knows not the roads."

As he went in and lighted his lantern, she continued to listen; and clear though faint came the sound of music from the same place. And now and then as little bursts became clearer, it seemed as if the melody was such a one as comes from strings.

In a moment, Father Michal was beside her, and they set out on the path that crossed the old ruined court and went by steps and slopes to the path below. The path attained, they followed it up an incline for a short distance, Anusia leading her companion and then turning off to the left across the hard-crusted snow.

He caught up to her in an instant, and the music that had seemed to be coming closer and closer as they went along now ceased for a moment. Anusia stood still until it was resumed. Some uncertainty as to its location because of the curious sound effects created by the ledges and projecting stones led her astray for a time, but she had fixed the point of issuance firmly in her senses, and when the notes struck her ear again she found herself not far off the path.

Quicker and quicker she went, and beside her, Michal, who already was breathing fast, panted, "Careful now." And

then she saw that suddenly the world had come to an end. The vision before them was no longer snow or cliff or crag; it was the open blackness of space, pierced here and there with pinpoints of light from distant villages.

The music was now directly beneath them, and she could catch the sound of a bow drawn over strings. It was a violin, then, that someone was playing somewhere down in the darkness.

"There," she exclaimed, guiding Michal's hand until it pointed toward the spot. "It is below us. Do you hear?"

He waited, and then he said No.

"Someone is still playing, down among the cliffs."

He drew her back from the edge of the sheer precipice that dropped away hundreds of feet to the plain, and then threw himself flat upon his stomach with his head protruding beyond the edge: "Hallo—hallo—hallo."

"*Sauvez-moi!*" The words, called out by a boy, floated up.

Father Michal was about to shout back "What?" when suddenly the significance of the cry came to him. The words were French—the language he had studied so long with his tutor. The language that all educated Poles spoke in the old days. He realized at that moment that the boy had said, "Save me!"

"Where are you?" Michal asked the question slowly in French as the words came back to him.

"Here—on a shelf about twelve feet below the top. I was lost in the dark and fell over."

"How long can you hold on?"

"I don't know. The ledge is narrow, and my feet and body are cramped. I dare not sit down for fear of slipping."

Michal was silent for a few moments, but his mind was picturing great thoughts. Huge dynamos never worked more powerfully; armies on the march never created such motion; in those moments, he ran over every possibility that the situation offered.

"How old are you?"

"Twelve years."

"How much do you weigh?"

"Ninety pounds."

To himself: "Ninety pounds. I think I can make it." Then aloud: "Hold tight for ten minutes, and I'll be back with a rope."

"Yes, monsieur. Thank God, and praise to you. I'm tired, but I can wait that long."

It had been Michal's idea to go to the village for help. At least Goral Jacek would come back. But that would have taken hours, and the boy on the narrow ledge might have lost his balance or plunged into the abyss to relieve cramped muscles. No, there was no time for that. He must do something himself . . .

If these old muscles will only hold out, he thought as he rose up and went back to Anusia. "*Attendez, attendez,*" he shouted, and then whispered to her: "You stay here. Do not move from your place; but tell me everything that happens below."

After a time that must have seemed like ages to a boy who was standing on a very small ledge and for whom a single shifting of a foot might have been fatal, he returned with a long coil of rope. To one end was attached a belt—the rescue rope used by mountaineers. The belt is girded firmly about the body by the person who is to be lifted up, and then at a given signal he is hoisted to safety. Old Michal had rescued other men from like predicaments in the past, but he had always

had Jacek's help. To do it alone was a different matter, especially at night and on the edge of a ravine where the rock might sever the rope at any second.

He fastened one end of the rope tightly around an upright stone a short distance from the edge. Then approaching the abyss, he shouted down that he was lowering the rope and that the boy was to buckle the end of the belt around his waist.

"Now courage," shouted the old man in French. "I am going to haul you up. But you will be dead weight unless you can help me by getting a toehold here and there on the cliff."

"God save you, monsieur. Shout when you are ready."

He led Anusia to the place where the rope passed over the brink and began its descent. "Here you must help me, Anusia," said Father Michal. "I have brought this piece of leather from the house and have put it between the rope and the rock here so that the rock will not fray nor cut the rope. If it does, then the boy will fall to his death. Here is what I want you to do. Will you remember?"

"I will, Father Michal."

"Then keep your hands on that leather and be sure that it does not slip when I pull on the rope. If the rope cuts through it or if the stone pierces the leather, try to move it under the rope so there will always be a whole piece of leather between the rope and the stone."

"Yes, Father Michal." And she fell on her knees at the precipice edge and felt the rope being drawn up tight by Michal, who was now taking up slack.

"Ready."

"Ready" was echoed from below.

"Then, with God," and the old man, with his hands grasping knots he had tied in the rope, gave a great heave and pulled up as much as he could in one mighty tug. The perspiration stood out on his head in beads and trickled down his neck. But with this effort he had raised the boy some three or four feet. Then, still keeping the line taut, he encircled the stone with the slack and braced himself for another haul. This time it came easier, for the boy had found a place in which to rest a toe, and some three or four feet more came up. This slack also he wound about the rock and rested a moment, though he could not remain motionless as long as he might wish since the thought of the helpless being dangling at the other end was constantly in his eyes. He hauled again and again, and now Anusia could make out the top of the boy's head as he neared the edge of the precipice.

One more great effort would do it, but as the boy was rising for the last interval and seeking to get another hold upon the rocks and pull himself to safety, Anusia felt with horror that the rope had cut clear through the leather. How it happened she could not see; but it was caused either by the rope's slipping away from the smooth stretch Father Michal had chosen or else an unexpected tug had sliced through it swiftly. And before she had a chance to grasp at the leather and work it back into place, it fell completely severed on either side of the rope and was lost from her fingers in the darkness.

There was no time to think; there was time only for action. Stripping off her leather jacket in an incredibly swift motion, she rolled it up and slipped it along the rope just below the edge until with her pushing and the hauling of the man at the rope's end it worked up into place and raised the rope above the sharp blade of the rock. And she was just in time for this as well, for the jagged edge had already torn

loose several strands from the cord and was entering deeper and deeper each second. And now, as impulses like lightning flashes went up and down through her body, the rope leaped away from the rock, there was another heave and a scramble and the boy, gasping for breath, crawled over the brink and lay upon the stones like a lifeless thing.

But old Michal was upon him in an instant. Though panting himself, suffering in every muscle and nerve from the effort that he had made, he gave the boy the first necessary relief, which was to unbuckle the belt drawn to excruciating tightness by the upward pull and allow the air to filter into the lungs. This done he collapsed and fell to earth by the side of Anusia and the rescued boy.

For a moment they lay there. Anusia, however, was up quickly. The boy struggled to his feet next and began to feel around for the violin that he had strapped carefully to his back before he had given the signal to Michal to lift. Thank God, it was safe! Several times during the ascent he had thought of it and had kept his body facing the rocky cliff, knowing that if he swung about and his back struck against the rock, it would damage and perhaps splinter his beloved violin. And seeing that it was safe he began to embrace it and kiss it.

And well he might, for that violin had saved his life! It was only when his voice had failed him that he had turned to this instrument and at imminent risk of losing his balance had played and played away desperately, hoping that it would be heard.

"You have saved me!" he exclaimed, caressing and kissing the old man's hands. But Michal, rising, pointed to Anusia and said, "It is *she* who has saved you. Had she not put her cloak between the rope and the rock, the rope would have broken, and you would have been lost."

They were soon on the way to the little hut, with the starlight playing on the snow and the bells sounding from the distant villages.

"Noel," said the boy suddenly.

But they decided now not to linger in the cold, for the boy and Michal were weak from effort and shock, and Anusia had no jacket—the last heave having sent it rolling down over the cliffs. As the door closed upon them, they all sank down in chairs with sighs of relief and comfort at the glow of the fire and the room's genial warmth.

Anusia stared at the stranger, and the stranger stared first at her and then at the old man. Father Michal had caught his breath, but now he was still strangely excited, and the sight of the boy seemed to add to his excitement.

"What is your name, my lad?"

The boy was of medium height, slender, with dark hair and eyes and clad in dark clothing—all of which made his handsome white face stand out.

"Je m'appelle Stephan Brossecelle." ("My name is Stephan Brossecelle.")

"Where do you live?"

"My home was in the town of Quintin in France."

"And you are French?"

"My mother was French."

"How did you come here?"

"I was on my way to Poland. My parents have been dead many years, and I was bound over to a man who traveled from town to town with a motion picture show on a wagon. He beat me, and I hated him. I intended to run away a long time ago, but when we traveled from France to a small village in Czechoslovakia, I decided that now was my chance."

"Did you not know what risk it was in the middle of winter?"

"I did, but I had to leave that showman. I played for him afternoon and evening. We went to fairs and to markets. We played by roadsides and slept in barns and on benches in parks. I hated it all, and I hated my master."

A curious light had come into the old man's eyes. There was something in the face, in the voice of the boy that held him spellbound. He asked his questions with increasing eagerness.

"Why were you so anxious to come to Poland?"

"My father was a Pole."

"Yet you lived in France."

"He was a refugee. They raised a Polish regiment in Quintin, and while there he met my mother and fell in love with her."

Michal began to stride up and down the room; his body was swinging Polish fashion from right to left with excitement.

"Do you remember your father?"

"Not very well. He died when I was young."

"Did he never teach you Polish words?"

"Yes, some."

"Think of them. Can you remember them?"

"Yes." And the boy struggled with his memories. "He told me that when I should go back to Poland I was to find his village—I cannot remember the name. Yet, hold, he told me something to say. In Latin it was."

The air had suddenly become tense. Old Michal could scarcely control himself. "Say the words."

"They come slowly. The first word was *Silva*."

The face of Michal had become like the face of Moses when he came down from the mountain. It was white and pallid yet living and young and full of expression.

" '*Silva*' you say?"

"Yes. *Silva*." The boy suddenly felt himself subject to a gripping emotion. He looked into the old man's eyes.

"*Coronat?*"

"Yes," answered Stephan, astounded. "That was it. The next word was *aquas*."

Tears leaped into the old man's eyes. "In God's holy name, go on," he said. "The next word?"

"I have it all," said the boy, the whole line leaping into his mind: "*Silva coronat aquas, cingens latus omne.*"

"Your name you say was Brossecelle?" demanded Michal. "Did you never hear the name Broszewicz?"

"Yes," exclaimed the boy, "that was it. The other was French for the Polish name. That was my father's name. Yet he seldom used it in the French village."

"Can you remember more?"

The old man's emotion had stirred hidden memories in the boy. Words that his father had used five or six years before began to straggle into his consciousness.

"Yes. I remember. When I was a boy, he told me to come back to Poland someday—that the words that I have told you would give me friends. His people were all dead, he said. He had even been back to their old home since the war and found them gone. That was when the legions came in with Haller."

He ceased speaking, for the old man was sobbing like a child, and Anusia, scarce comprehending, stared at them both. At length, he raised his head from the table and, looking at the boy, said in a low tone, "Stefan Broszewicz, you are my own grandson. Your father was my son. The sentence that

he gave you was the motto of our house. It is this: 'A Wood Crowns the Waters, Surrounding One Side.' By this were the boundaries of our estate known of old, the wood and waters about it forming one side of the property and so named in Latin in the grant given by our king."

Then taking the lad in his arms, he kissed his forehead and his wrists saying the while: "I knew you when I first saw you," and "Christ sent you on His holy night." But ceasing for a while, he told the story to Anusia who had thought back over their talk earlier in the evening and had guessed a part of it. And all the while the bells rang out for joy in the villages, and men and women and children worshiped before the gleaming altars and cried out, "Peace on earth, good will to men!"

Eric Philbrook Kelly (1884–1960) was born in Amesbury, Massachusetts. He spent his academic career teaching English and journalism at Dartmouth College. Author of *The Trumpeter of Krakow* and *The Blacksmith of Vilno*. No other American writer has done more to bring Polish history to life for American readers.

Little Cherry's Star

G. M. Farley

A blizzard raged outside the little isolated cabin on the Western plains. Mama grew weaker by the hour, and Papa was somewhere, they knew not where, in the fierce storm. Their firewood was secured behind towering drifts of show. The house grew steadily colder.

But little Cherry still believed . . .

* * * * *

Little Cherry was cold. She wrapped her clothes closer about her small body and shivered. She remembered how nice the warm summer days had been, how comfortable October's Indian summer, and how nice the cabin had felt before Papa had saddled his horse and ridden away. He had hugged her close, had kissed Mama, and promised to be back within a week. That was more than a week ago now, and he hadn't returned. The supply of firewood that Papa had carried into the house had nearly vanished. And now Mama wasn't feeling well.

Outside, as dusk began to deepen towards night, the blizzard continued to rage over whitened Western plains. Huge drifts of snow had piled around the cabin, blocking the path to the stacks of firewood in the shed by the barn. And the wind moaned fiercely around the cabin, adding to the misery of its occupants.

"Mama," Cherry said softly, "why doesn't Papa come home?"

She knew the answer would be the same as it had been every time she had asked the question. Somehow, though, there was some consolation in her mother's reply.

"Soon now. He's probably having trouble in this storm." Mama's voice sounded weak as she wet her lips to continue. "The horse can't travel fast in such a wind, and the drifts must be up to his chest. But don't fret now. Papa will be home soon."

"But Mama, he said he would be home for Christmas, and . . . and tomorrow's Christmas, isn't it, Mama?" Little Cherry's voice almost trembled. She could never let that happen. Mama didn't seem to be feeling well enough to help a little girl who was crying, so Cherry had to be brave now—at least until Papa returned. Then everything would be all right again.

"Yes, dear, tomorrow is Christmas."

"And, Mama, he promised to have a tree with pretty things on it, didn't he? . . . And, he said I might have a doll too." Cherry suddenly wished she hadn't said that. It had put a strange, sad expression on Mama's face. She would change the subject and help Mama forget.

"Tell me about the Baby Jesus, Mama," she requested as she sat down on the side of the bed.

"All right, honey, but first put some wood on the fire. Just one piece. Then we will still have some for tonight and tomorrow. There! Now come back and sit by me while I tell you."

Cherry listened intently to her mother's weak voice as she told her a story that was undoubtedly being repeated that evening all over the world. Little children in fine warm homes would thrill to the same story. Children in warm climates and children sitting before roaring log fires watching the dancing flames for a while and then returning their gaze to the tree so beautifully decorated and aglow with burning candles. Those children couldn't dream that in a cold, dark cabin on the Western plains a shivering girl's eyes twinkled as she listened again to the story of a new star in the heavens, of angels singing to shepherds, and of a baby sleeping in a manger. Then Mama had finished.

"But, Mama, why did Jesus leave heaven to be a baby?" Cherry asked.

"Well, Cherry, I don't really know how to tell you. I . . . I suppose I can put it like this: Heaven is just filled with wonderful and beautiful things for people like you and me. For everyone, in fact. He came so someday we could go there; to a place where there will never be snow or wind or cold. Papa will always be with us, and you will never be hungry there, either."

"But, Mama, why can't we have some of those things here? We can, can't we?"

"Well, honey . . . Yes, I believe we can."

"Then why don't we ask Jesus to give us some of them? We can do that, can't we, Mama?"

"Yes, of course we can. We will just pray and ask Him to do it. You can kneel right here, and I will hold your hand while you pray."

Cherry's prayer was brief and simple as only a child's prayer can be. She prayed it by herself as Mama listened. In the increasing darkness she didn't see the tears on Mama's cheeks.

"Dear Jesus," she prayed, "Mama has just told me all the good things You have for us. She said if I would ask You for some of them You would send them to us. Papa is gone, dear Jesus, and Mama is worried about him. Won't you please send him home to us? And Jesus, send us some food and some wood and . . . and . . . and a doll too. Amen."

A child's faith had sent words before the throne of Him who is eternal. The prayer was heard, and even though Cherry and Mama knew it not, angels were already busy with the answer.

In the cabin, darkness was held back only by the feeble flames in the fireplace. The chill that had invaded the cabin days before still prevailed. Death could only try to reach the mother and daughter now. It wouldn't succeed, for a child's faith had moved the hand of God.

"Mama," Cherry's voice interrupted the wail of the wind, "what would have happened if there hadn't been a star when Jesus was born?"

"I don't really know, Cherry. I suppose the wise men wouldn't have found Jesus. Why do you ask?"

"Because I think I would like to put a star in our window like God put in heaven on the first Christmas Eve. Would it be alright, Mama, if I used your candle? You don't ever use it, and it would make it a little more like Christmas."

"Why certainly," Mama replied, her voice sounding soft. "Just be careful not to set it where the flame will touch the logs."

And so it was that long after Cherry had gone to sleep beside her mother and as her mother listened to the gale that appeared to be gradually diminishing, a knock sounded at the door. For a moment the mother lay still, watching the flickering candle. Then suddenly hope leaped within her breast. Could this be Jeff returning at last? The thought gave her strength, and she slowly arose from the bed. The knock came again, this time accompanied by a voice—a strange voice.

In the muffled tones of the voice she heard her name, and then another name . . . the name of their nearest neighbor. Her heart leaped again as she recognized the voice of Lincoln Bowers from the adjoining ranch . . . but his home was at least five miles away. Something must be wrong; something must have happened to Jeff. Fear flooded her heart.

Slowly she made her way to the door and opened it to disclose not one but two snow-covered men. Behind them stood their horses silhouetted faintly against the snow. "Won't you come in please?" she invited.

"What a night!" Mr. Bowers said. "I don't ever remember a Christmas Eve as bad as this one. Say, this place is almost as cold as outside! Where's the wood?"

Realizing the situation, Mr. Bowers had his companion bring wood from the shed and get a hot fire blazing. Then he turned again to Mama. "Now," he said, "I have some news for you. You are a very fortunate woman. Your husband is at my ranch. He stumbled in there late this afternoon just about all in. Seems his horse had walked into a snowdrift and fell with him. Crippled the horse, so Jeff had to walk through that blizzard. He was packing his saddle and a bag of Christmas things. Well, he got lost and finally wandered into my place about half dead. He nearly froze to death."

"Thank God he is alive!" Mama's voice trembled with emotion.

"He finally managed to tell us what he was trying to do." Mr. Bowers said gruffly. It was obvious he'd been touched by Mama's outburst. "He was trying to get these things here for Christmas. Said Little Cherry's heart was set on a doll in the morning. I figure a couple days of rest and care, and he can come home."

Mama wept softly and in her heart thanked God for His goodness. She had feared the worst, even though she had kept her fears hidden from her little daughter.

Cherry stirred in her sleep. Outside the wind seemed to envelop the cabin in a new fury. The horses stirred restlessly near the door.

Mr. Bowers continued, "Here's the bag of Christmas things Jeff was packing, and right here on top of it is a doll for the girl. We tried to get a little tree to fix for her, but the storm was so bad we sort of got turned around. Fact is, in all the drifts, and with the snow flying as it is, we didn't know just for sure where we were going.

"We were heading right on by the cabin when we saw your light. If that candle hadn't been in your window, we might easily have been in a worse fix than Jeff was."

The candle! Mama had forgotten the candle Cherry had placed in the window. It had likely saved two lives and had made it possible for them to have a Christmas. Without the candle she wouldn't have known that her husband was safe. Without the candle there wouldn't be a Christmas tree near the sleeping girl's bed—a tree the men found near the cabin before they vanished into the stormy night.

Later, as Mama placed the doll on a chair near the tree, the words Cherry had spoken that evening came to her: "I would like to put a star in our window tonight, just like God put in heaven on the first Christmas Eve."

And then suddenly it seemed to Mama that she could almost hear an angelic host hovering near the little cabin, singing words that had thrilled both child and adult down through the years ever since a little Baby slept in a manger at Bethlehem of Judah: "Glory to God in the highest, and on earth, peace and good will toward men."

Christmas had come to Little Cherry.

G. M. Farley (1927–1992) was born in West Virginia. Besides holding pastorates and administrative posts in Pentecostal churches, he was also a prolific writer and scholar, and one of the world's leading authorities on the life and works of the frontier writer Zane Grey.

The Christmas Kink

Lucille Adams

For thirty long years now she'd yearned for a Christmas unaccompanied by rushing around and exhaustion. Now she had it—and she was anything but sure she liked it.

* * * * *

This was the Christmas she had been looking forward to for thirty years—Christmas with no rush, no exhaustion. This year there would be time to find the Christmas spirit. Not since she and Jim were married and Peggy and Beth were nonexistent had Margaret been able to walk out of an orderly kitchen at two o'clock on Christmas Eve.

The whole house was orderly. She glanced around approvingly as she walked into the living room, where she looked into the mirror above the fireplace. Even her hair was in order.

Other years she had rushed from kitchen to living room, from the turkey to the tree Jim was trimming. When she happened to look into the mirror, her hair would be flying, and always there was a smudge of flour on her forehead. Jim's tools would be in the middle of the floor and he would be on a ladder, while Beth hopped around, telling him how to arrange the lights. Even last Christmas, two days before her wedding, Beth had helped with the tree. Maybe she and Bob would have a little tree for their baby this year, young as he was.

The girls would laugh if they could see the little tree that Jim had trimmed in fifteen minutes. It was on the desk, and beside it were Christmas gifts to be delivered.

The house seemed terribly quiet. Margaret was glad when she heard Jim coming in.

"Well, what do you know? Christmas Eve, and you're sitting around with nothing to do!" he remarked.

Jim is still handsome, Margaret thought, *in spite of his dark-rimmed glasses and gray-streaked hair.* "This is the year I'm playing lady," she said. "Remember?"

"For my money you're *always* a lady." He handed her some envelopes. "The postman gave me these."

"More Christmas cards. And the bank statement!" said Margaret.

"Here, I'll take that. Don't want you to see what your Christmas present cost," exclaimed Jim.

Dear Jim. She shouldn't have this queer, empty feeling now that he was home.

"Do you still want to deliver those packages?" He nodded toward the desk.

"I'd like to. I've always wanted to deliver our gifts the day before Christmas instead of the day *after*."

"I'll change and be with you in a jiffy."

Alone, Margaret put an album of carols on the record player. She had always wanted to have time to sit down and listen to the Christmas music at her leisure, for she had long had a theory that somewhere within those carols lay the

Christmas spirit, if only a person had time to listen! With the first notes of "Adeste Fideles" she relaxed in her chair.

She wondered what Peggy and Mike were doing—and the two boys. Probably Mike was fixing the tree while Peggy worked on the turkey. This was the first time the boys hadn't spent Christmas with Grandma and Grandpa. If it weren't for the work, she would have liked to have them in the house right now. Suddenly, she was conscious of a voice singing, "I'll Be Home for Christmas." That one she could do without! She leaned over and turned off the record as Jim appeared in the door.

"Getting homesick for the kids?" he asked, looking at her closely.

"Oh, no," she assured him halfheartedly. "Just enjoying the carols. If you're ready, let's go."

"OK. I'll put the packages in the car."

"Seems good to have time to wish our friends Merry Christmas," Margaret said when Jim parked at the Andersons'.

Inside there wasn't much chance to say "Merry Christmas" or anything else. Young Bob Anderson and his wife, with their three small children, had just arrived for the holidays. Lois came in from the kitchen with her youngest grandchild in her arms. "When will Peggy and her family get here?" she asked, hugging the baby to her.

"They aren't coming this year," Margaret told her. "They bought a television set, so they can't afford the trip home."

"What a shame," Lois said. "But Beth and Bob and the baby will come, won't they?"

"You forget that Bob isn't his own boss," Margaret replied—more sharply than she intended. "With only five days off at Christmastime, they couldn't possibly come home, unless they'd fly—and they can't do that on a sergeant's pay."

Jim and Mr. Anderson emerged from the back of the house, and Margaret said they must run along. As Jim backed the car out of the Anderson driveway, he said, "Nice their boy and his family could get home, isn't it?"

"Hmm—looked like a lot of work," Margaret replied.

"It is a lot of work for a woman," Jim agreed.

"No more than for you. Aren't you glad you don't have to put up a big tree—and get a kink in your back the way you used to?"

"Yeah," Jim agreed hesitantly. "I guess we both deserve a rest. Tomorrow we'll eat downtown. You'll have your turkey served in style, and I'll be sitting across from you with nary an aching muscle."

They finished their calls in a surprisingly short time. Everyone seemed too busy for more than a brief greeting. It was only four o'clock when they returned home.

"Guess I'll get something to drink," Jim said, heading for the kitchen.

Margaret walked over to the record player. Maybe she'd try the carols again. When it came to "I'll Be Home for Christmas," she jumped the needle over to the next piece!

The music filled the room. Somehow, Margaret's eyes dimmed. She didn't really want to listen to carols—she wanted to hear her daughters' voices. She wanted to hold Beth's baby in her arms. She couldn't fool herself any longer. If she could have her children home for Christmas again, she wouldn't care how much work she'd have to do!

The doorbell jerked her out of her thoughts, and when she opened the front door, a grinning Western Union boy handed her a telegram. She ripped open the yellow envelope. Probably a greeting from a relative. But when she read it, she ran to the kitchen!

"Jim! Jim!" she shrieked. "Listen to this. Beth and Bob are coming home! And the baby! They'll be at the airport at 6:45. Isn't it wonderful?" And again she couldn't hold back the silly tears.

"It's great!" Jim took off his glasses and brushed a knuckle across his eyes.

"Put your coat on," Margaret directed. "We'll have to leave right away, so we'll have time to stop and get a turkey!"

"Yeah—a big one!" Jim exclaimed. "Come on, let's get to the market before it closes!"

The phone was ringing as they returned from the market, their arms loaded with sacks of groceries. Margaret ran to answer it. Clay City! Who in the world? Then she heard Peggy's voice. "Hello, Mom? We've decided to come home for Christmas after all. We're driving and should be in about eight."

Margaret turned from the phone, her eyes shining. "It was Peggy, Jim. They're coming too! Driving. Oh, Jim, isn't it perfect?"

"It's great!" Jim said as he put down the bulging bags he was holding. "Guess I'd better try to rustle up a bigger tree for the boys."

"Yes, that little one would never do," Margaret agreed. "You take care of the tree. I'll make piecrust and stuff the turkey before we go to the airport."

Margaret had just finished when Jim called her to look at the tree. "It's beautiful!" she exclaimed. "The prettiest tree we've ever had!"

She stepped over his tools in the middle of the floor and glanced into the mirror. Her hair was a fright! Jim got down from the ladder holding his back.

"Your Christmas kink?" she asked.

"Yeah. Wouldn't seem like Christmas without it." He put his arms around her.

"Jim," Margaret said thoughtfully, "I wonder how it happened that the youngsters found they could afford to come home after all!"

"I wonder," Jim said, not too excitedly. Gently he brushed the flour off her forehead, and Margaret looked into his face, and saw the twinkle in his eyes.

"You're an old fraud!" she told him. He kissed her then, and suddenly she knew that the spirit of Christmas was all around them.

Lucille Adams wrote for magazines during the second half of the twentieth century.

Flight Before Christmas

John Scott Douglas

"Never again," the young Alaskan pilot vowed, "will I pilot another plane! That last flight cured me. If I can't be sure the lives of passengers are safe in my care—and I see now I can't—then I'll let others fly who can."

Hope, the lovely nurse, now looked at him as someone she no longer knew.

* * * * *

The cabin monoplane rocked violently, struck by a sudden sharp gust of wind. Lane Ramsey tensed at the controls. The Deception Bay emergency landing field was blue-white under the steely arctic sky.

The bay had been given its name in the day of sailing ships. It wasn't by chance that the place had been called Deception Bay; the winds here were treacherous.

Nerves taut, Lane expected the gust to die. If anything, it stiffened. Mistrustfully, he nosed down. Then, moments later he experienced relief as he started to level out the monoplane. Its ski runners were striking out for a gliding surface when the fickle wind abruptly failed. Paralyzing moment! There was no time to correct for the breathless calm. Robbed of support, the plane dropped like a stone.

Lane snapped off his ignition switch before the plane jarred. The nose-heavy ship fell on the upcurve of its runners. They plowed crunching snow in a wild flurry. Wood splintered and then clashed with metal. Automatically, Lane threw up a hand to protect his face as the monoplane nosed up. A split second later, lightning streaked across his vision.

* * * * *

A nurse was bandaging Lane's head when he opened his eyes. For several blank moments the girl's vivid blue eyes and almost Scandinavian blondness stirred no memory, although, on his infrequent trips into the Arctic Circle, Lane had always looked forward to seeing Hope Loring. They had gone to the same small school in Fairbanks. Accident had placed them on the same boat going south; Hope leaving Alaska to study nursing, Lane to study aeronautics.

The familiar interior of Ole Peterson's trading post finally enabled him to orient himself. He was lying on the counter.

Hope smiled. "How do you feel?"

"I have a headache built for a whale," Lane muttered. "But I don't matter. How are my five passengers?"

"They're coming along fine. Now be quiet."

Lane struggled to sit up. Pain darted from a dozen points. Dizzy, he sank back onto the counter, stifling a groan.

"Tell me the truth, Hope! Have I hurt any of my passengers?"

Her lips pursed. "You did all you could, Lane, by cutting the switch so that there was no explosion when your plane

cracked up. Everyone knows how tricky the winds are here."

He tried to move his left arm, and winced at the pain. For the first time, he realized it was in a splint. Impressions were still a little blurred. He lay still, breathing heavily.

"Lie quietly, and I'll tell you everything," Hope said. "Your arm was broken, and Mr. Peterson helped me set it. Two of your passengers are only bruised. Another passenger has a broken leg; still another, a broken finger. We have set the bones; there should be no trouble."

"But the fifth passenger?" Lane asked anxiously.

"Mr. Graham has a slight concussion. There's no doctor nearer than Point Happy, but Mr. Peterson has had a great deal of practical experience in the forty years he's had this trading post."

"Has a doctor been sent for?"

"Joe Ladue has gone with dogs, but it's three days each way."

Six days! As soon as his head cleared a bit, Lane looked into Hope's room, now a temporary hospital for old Mr. Graham. The other passengers had been dispatched to stay with other settlers. Graham lay deathly still.

Night brought little change in the unconscious man, but his breathing became more labored. Hope's blue eyes were shadowed each time she took his pulse. All night she remained on duty. She refused to let Lane relieve her. Morning brought no change. Then Lane's strong rugged face became stern.

"You must get some sleep, Hope," he said. "My throbbing head won't let me rest. I'll tell you if there's any change."

* * * * *

For five days and nights they fought side by side to save the injured prospector. Then his pulse grew stronger, and presently he noticed his surroundings. His blue eyes were puzzled. Her voice not quite steady, Hope told him what had happened.

"Land sakes! I been makin' a reg'lar nuisance of myself, miss."

Lane Ramsey's eyes stung. Relief swept over him. He had not realized how heavily his passenger's accident had weighed on him. His responsibility! But not until Joe Ladue brought the doctor the next day did he feel entirely relieved.

The doctor made a careful examination and then laughed. "I guess you've had better help than I could give you. The other passengers need me more than you do, Graham."

"Sure," said the old-timer. "That's what I've been telling them."

Lane donned his heavy parka and mukluks and strode out to the emergency landing field. During his spare time he had superintended the dragging of the damaged plane into a small hangar that had been erected by one of the Alaskan airlines. Using Hope's shortwave radio set, he had ordered replacement parts in the event another plane took a flight this far north before winter closed in. But he had not entered the hangar since placing his plane there—a strange thing, considering that his whole interest had been aviation since he had gone to the States to get his training.

An hour later, he glanced up from the examination of his plane to see Hope entering the hangar.

"Dr. Willett has examined all my patients except you," she said, smiling. "I suppose you're anxious to get your parts so you can be off."

He raised brooding eyes. "No, I've flown for the last time."

She started. "But your arm won't—"

"Not my arm," he interrupted. "It's what nearly happened to Mr. Graham."

"But, Lane, that wasn't your fault." Her voice was warmly sympathetic. "The winds here have always been treacherous. No one blames you."

"I do," he said bleakly. "Always before it's been a game, trying to beat the elements. That's all right for me, but now I realize that I have no right to jeopardize the lives of my passengers. This has—well—knocked the confidence out of me."

Hope gave him a strange, probing glance. "You've lost your nerve?"

"I—I don't know, but I won't fly again. I'll fix up the plane. Then I'll radio the line that used to employ me before I bought this bus, and offer it for sale. If they'll buy it, I'll have them fly in a pilot and let him take the job out."

"Lane, you're letting a near fatality blind you to what Alaska was before there were planes. Then men went snow-blind on the trail, froze to death, got lost. Pilots like you have lessened the risk. You can't hope to wipe it out entirely when the forces of cold, darkness, and snow are all against you. But you've helped. That's something."

His strong face was grim. "I've thought of all that."

"Then think of something else," she cried spiritedly. "Someone has said, 'Never be so mad as to doubt yourself.' I've admired you, Lane, until the last three minutes. Now I'm beginning to believe you're suffering from a bad case of self-pity."

"Thank you," he said in a brittle voice. "You don't understand at all. I'd go up this minute alone, but never again with a passenger."

"Then why have someone else fly your plane out?"

He winced. "If I ever got back of the controls, I'd weaken. I'd fly again; and perhaps next time I'd have a spill my passengers wouldn't get out of so luckily."

"You're letting fear overturn what confidence you have built," Hope said. "If you think you don't have the skill to fly in Alaska, who *is* qualified? Last time Greg Martin flew in here, he said, 'I don't mind admitting that on some of these flights I just about break from the strain of wondering whether I'm going to get through. Low clouds, snow and ice, storms! We aren't all Lane Ramseys. He'd go through the worst blizzard and never turn a hair. The line lost something when it lost him.' I've heard others talk like that too, and yet you're quitting!"

"Yes. I've risked the lives of my passengers for the last time. The others flyers have called me 'Timetable Ramsey' in fun. Little do they know! My knees were shaking when I got in from some of my trips. Naturally, I tried to keep from showing it."

Her eyes became chilly. In a coldly impersonal voice, she said, "The doctor would like to examine your arm now, Lane."

There was a lump in his throat as he walked stiffly back to the trading post. How could he make Hope understand? She was the one person he wanted most to understand!

Something had happened to Lane Ramsey during those five days beside the bed of old Graham. For the first time the great responsibility of his work weighed on him. It was true that more lives might be lost by dog sled. But that was impersonal, while the kind-faced old man fighting for life was as real as his right hand. Graham had a wife back in Skagway, and it was for her that he was once more going into the

interior. Gold had been discovered at Point Happy, and the old man wanted to have his claim staked for the spring rush. If he had not lived, Lane would never have forgiven himself. That kindly old face would have haunted his memory for the rest of his life.

* * * * *

After the doctor had left accompanied by the two uninjured prospectors, the atmosphere became strained. Hope treated Lane like an utter stranger and spoke to him only when absolutely necessary. The Petersons sensed trouble and attempted to heal the breach. Not knowing the nature of the trouble, however, they failed.

Uncomfortable at the trading post, Lane moved in with one of the settlers. He saw Hope only when she examined his arm, visited one of her other patients, or passed down the street on dogsled on her way to visit an Eskimo family nearby who needed her help.

Then Greg Martin flew in a man and his wife along with the parts Lane needed to repair his plane. Lane discussed the sale of his plane. Much surprised, Greg admitted the line needed another cabin monoplane to take care of the spring business.

"And we could use another pilot as good as you are," he said. "Think it over, Lane. You can't keep a good flier down, and you'll be itching to fly by spring."

Hope Loring unexpectedly announced that she would fly to Point Happy as soon as Greg's plane was refueled. And Greg took off with his three passengers.

Lane's throat was tight with unhappiness those next few weeks. The weather became worse; storms sweeping across the Arctic Ocean, rattling the trading post, pounding the small dwellings huddled closely together. Sometimes he could barely fight his way to the heated hangar where he worked on his plane.

Then, all too soon, the plane was repaired, and there was nothing to occupy his mind. In desperation, he began to study the books on radio that, in her haste to depart, Hope had left behind. Soon he was able to talk to amateur operators as far away as Seattle, and sometimes farther, when conditions were not too adverse. Sometimes, too, he communicated with Hope Loring at Point Happy, but never by a single word did she suggest that she had forgiven him his attitude.

Dr. Willett called regularly at a certain time each day to receive the scant news from Deception Bay. Then influenza broke out among the Eskimos there. At one time, three-fourths of the settlers were down with flu. The Petersons worked night and day to do what they could, and Lane helped too.

One day, Hope inquired over the radio, "Has Dr. Willett arrived yet?"

It was the first time Lane had any inkling that the medical missionary had left Point Happy to help them. Storms raged across the snow-blanketed tundra. Was it possible for Dr. Willett to get through? He arrived that day, riding the runners of his sled.

With his help, the cases began to improve. In a week, Lane knew that they had passed the crisis. And then, the day before Christmas, he went to the radio at the usual hour to communicate with Point Happy.

"Lane," said the familiar voice, "the radio set is in a tent.

Fire broke out last night. Point Happy has been burned to the ground. You know how close together the buildings were. We saved what we could, but we're short of blankets, short of food. I know no planes can get through the storms, but could Joe Ladue bring us blankets and a tent or so? We're building snow houses.

"And by the way, the children are brokenhearted. We'd promised them a Santa Claus."

Lane was stunned when he turned away from the radio. Point Happy in ruins! Insufficient blankets, insufficient food! Men, women, and children threatened by exposure while snow houses were being hastily cut and built! What a Christmas outlook! Joe Ladue might get through in four days—if he was lucky. But how pitifully little he could transport by dog sled!

Lane broke the news to the Petersons. The old trader cried, his voice husky, "Blankets! Dey can have all I got. Yah! But how vill ve get dem to Point Happy?"

Bracing himself against the screaming wind, Lane walked down the street, looking for Dr. Willett. The doctor listened in silence to the sad news Lane had to tell him and then nodded. "We'll have to go by plane, Lane. There's only one pilot in Alaska I'd trust to make it through this storm. That's you."

Lane shook his head grimly.

"Listen," Doctor Willett said quietly, "the trouble with you, Lane, is that you're too sensitive. You think you should be infallible. No man is that, son. The doctor with that attitude would never take a case because he might fail. The engineer would never step into a locomotive because a switch might be turned the wrong way. The lifeguard would never attempt to save a drowning man. All we can do is our best.

For the rest, we must trust in God. If each of us can do our little bit, we have served; and the result of many a little is great accomplishment."

Lane stood rigid. "I hadn't thought of it that way," he said slowly.

* * * * *

The plane was but a red dot in the swirling flurries of snow when willing hands pushed it out of the hangar. It was loaded with blankets, food, and clothing for those in desperate circumstances at Point Happy, and Lane had taken all the precautions he could to ensure a safe flight.

Just before Lane took off, Ole Peterson discovered a box containing toys and masks. One of those masks would make a great St. Nick. There was a red costume, too, which Lane put on over his flying togs. Doing this seemed strange when the odds were so greatly against his ever reaching his destination. But Lane couldn't forget that the next day was Christmas and that Point Happy was full of homeless youngsters.

When he took off, the plane was tossed, buffeted, and pounded, until his body ached from the strain of fighting his controls. His eyes were continually on his blind-flying instruments. Afterwards, he was always to wonder how he got through the darkness, how he caught sight of the fire that the settlers had built, lighted when they heard the first faint buzzing of his motor above the shriek and bellow of the wind.

The first thing Lane did after landing was to slip on the Santa Claus mask. When he climbed down from his plane, the children crowded around him, laughing and yelling. Dr. Willett handed him the sack of toys, and Lane gravely

distributed them, asking each of the children whether he or she had been good and patting them when they said they had been. Never had Lane seen such gratitude as when the settlers glanced into the crowded interior of the plane and saw the warm blankets and clothing he had brought.

"Three cheers for Santa Claus!" yelled one bearded prospector, and the cheers were deafening.

Hope Loring gripped Lane's mittened hands a few minutes later and met his eyes. "Santa Claus," she said in a choked voice, "may I cheer too?"

———————

John Scott Douglas was one of America's most prolific authors of stories for young people during the first half of the twentieth century.

Denny's Christmas Revelation

Faith Freeborn Turner

It was the season of Christmas, but the ragged little paperboy had nothing with which to buy a present for his shivering mother. Since none of the hurrying shoppers seemed to care if he lived or if he died, he began to doubt the stories of the Christ baby in the Bible.

But someone was listening to the boy's sorrowful monologue by the store window.

* * * * *

This is one of the oldest stories in this collection, the language is a bit dated, the street dialect is not easy to follow—yet the message itself is so powerful that it has defied the odds by staying alive for more than a hundred years now.

Its time has come.

* * * * *

T'ain't right, I tell you. T'aint right." The thin, bony little figure shivered in the scant covering afforded by a ragged pair of too large trousers and a much-patched and faded-looking red sweater.

The thermometer pointed a silver arrow at ten degrees below zero. A chill, piercing wind, blown in from the harbor, caused many pedestrians to pull their great-coat collars high and set their hats a trifle lower over their ears. Soft, white drifts were piled along the curb, and the sidewalks were slippery and treacherous.

Down one of those icy walks, bare hands thrust deep into the pockets of the too large trousers, walked the boy in the faded red sweater.

He slithered through the throng on the crowded thoroughfare like an eel. He knew it was Christmas Eve, and he knew that the shop windows were gleaming with enchanting gifts and toys, but he shrugged his shoulders. What did that mean to him? Nothing.

"T'ain't right," he muttered. "All de swells worry about is gettin' sompin' better'n 'de other feller. Dey don't worry none about us paper kids. Guess Mom was wrong. Christmas is all wrong—t'ain't right de way things are done."

The ragged paperboy jostled through a richly clad group of women who stood admiring a beautifully decorated window, displaying expensive clothing for the season. "De swells like them dames get all de clo'es—clo'es dey don't need, when Mom's—" Tears filled the big blue eyes, and the brave little chin quivered. "*Mom is de best ever.* She ain't a dame—she's a real lady, 'n she's freezin' 'cause she ain't even got nuff clo'es to keep her warm."

As Denny, for such was his name, came to one of the last shop windows in the row, he paused a moment and gazed wistfully through the plate glass at the lovely clothes displayed there. Yes, it was still there, that beautiful, warm-looking blue sweater. Denny sighed, and a stray tear trickled down his thin cheek. "If Mom could only have dat dis winter, she wouldn't cough so much maybe," he said, talking aloud to himself. "I ain't got only 'nough dough to buy sompin' for her to eat, so I guess t'ain't no good ta look at it." The blue eyes feasted on the warm wooly garment. They didn't look once at the smaller sweater for a boy his size. Denny's love for his mother had blotted out all thoughts of self.

As he gazed into the window, all the while muttering to himself, a fur-clad figure stood near, apparently interested in window-shopping. In reality the girl was listening carefully to the ragged boy's soliloquy.

"Wouldn't it be swell doe if Mom could be a' wearin' dat sweater ternight? Den maybe like dem times she tells about when she was in de country where folks know about de true Christmas spirit, as Mom's says, an' dey'd go carolin' at night ter people's houses, maybe somebody'd carol for Mom at our shack." The boy gulped. "T'ain't no use ter wish or whine. I guess der wasn't any baby born in de manger. Least-wise, nobody remembers Him. Dey are too busy gettin' sompin', I reckons. Dey don't sing dem 'Silent Night' songs for such as us—dat's only for de swells. Well, if I don't get my papers and work hard, Mom won't even have any supper."

With one last look at the sweater, Denny turned

and swung down the street at such a pace that the fur-clad figure following could scarce keep him in sight.

At the *Gazette* office, Denny got his papers and was soon standing on a busy corner, crying his wares. Back in the office, Phyllis Winslow stopped at the editor's desk. Upon getting the desired information as to Denny's name and whereabouts, she hurried back to the shop on Fifth Avenue. The clerk was soon busy gathering presents for the parcel. Not only the coveted blue sweater but house slippers, hose, a warm knitted dress, and several dainty luxuries went into the package. Then another package was made. Into it went a sweater, boots, trousers, warm hood and mittens, and last of all the toys and games that delight the heart of any boy.

Finally, the shopping was completed, even to a well-filled sack of fruits and candies. Phyllis hailed a taxi and gave the street number given her by the girl at the *Gazette* office. The cab eventually halted before a tiny, ramshackle building on the far side of the city. In spite of the poor district and the ramshackle house, Phyllis noted patched yet neat curtains hung at the window. In answer to her knock, a frail-looking woman, who must at one time have been very beautiful, appeared. "Is this where Denny Williams lives?" questioned Phyllis.

"Yes, won't you come in?" The one room, though very bare of furnishings and cold from the fierce wind outside, was neat and clean. In answer to the woman's questioning look, Phyllis explained, "I've brought you a few things, Mrs. Williams—not much, but perhaps it will help Denny to know that there are still a few who remember the birth of the Babe in the manger and who have the real Christmas spirit. Goodbye."

Before the astonished woman could speak, Phyllis opened the door, ran down the boardwalk, and entered the waiting cab.

When Mrs. Williams turned back into the room, she noticed bundles and packages stacked on the doorsteps. The driver had placed there the things Phyllis had purchased earlier that evening.

A lump filled Mrs. Williams' throat as she gazed down upon them. God had answered her prayer. She had trusted He would, for she knew that Denny's childish faith was wavering. Now he would believe the story of Jesus that she had learned as a little girl and had tried so hard to get Denny to understand. She began to unwrap the parcels, one at a time.

When Denny, low in spirits, pushed open the door of his home an hour later, he could hardly believe his eyes. In the only rocking chair they possessed sat his mother, smiling, and—yes—she did have on the blue sweater of the shop window.

"Mom, what—where! Dat sweater—How'd you get it, and the oranges and candy? Am I seein' things or what?"

"No, Denny, dear, your vision is correct." Mrs. Williams drew her brave little paper lad close to her and told him the story.

Outside the stars were shining brightly. The beautiful eastern star was strangely bright as the Bethlehem story was related again. And Denny's blue eyes were tearful as he exclaimed, "Mom, I was wrong. Dat Babe in the manger really *did* live, and His Spirit, as you say, makes de swells have a heart after all. Tell me more about—"

His words were cut short as, suddenly at the tiny window, a chorus of clear, lilting voices broke out—full and throbbing with the beauty and passion of the words they sang:

O little town of Bethlehem
    How still we see thee lie,
Above thy deep and dreamless sleep
    The silent stars go by.
But in thy dark streets shineth
    The everlasting light;
The hopes and fears of all the years
    Are met in thee tonight.

They sang the remaining verses of that song and then followed it with other songs of that wondrous night.

Finally the voices swung into the beautiful words of "Silent Night." Reverently and softly they sang each verse. The last word died away in the stillness of the night as the group of young people quietly made their way to the home of Phyllis Winslow.

As we take one more peep into the one-room home, we see Mrs. Williams sitting quietly in her chair. Her face is shining with a new light as she raises tear-stained cheeks to heaven. Denny, kneeling at his mother's knee, looks long into her face, then says in a grave voice, "Mom, ain't it queer? I feel now somehow like de swells ain't swells, and me—I'm not just a paper kid, but we're all de same like de shepherds and wise men dey was singin' about as we all worship de Babe in de manger—our Jesus, our King."

————————

Faith Freeborn Turner wrote around the turn of the twentieth century.

The Belated Christmas Train

William McGinnies

Every year I search for memorable short, short Christmas stories. Most of the time I fail to find them.

But this year, reading a hundred-plus-year-old Ladies' Home Journal, *God gifted me with what I'd been seeking for so long.*

* * * * *

All the forenoon of the day before Christmas the train had been plowing across the desert, winding through canyons, or climbing mountains on its way east across Arizona and New Mexico. It stopped for dinner where it should have stopped for breakfast, and it was a sullen-looking lot of passengers that left the cars for the dining room.

Dinner didn't brighten them up much, and they returned to their cars complaining bitterly of the luck that made their train late this particular day when all were anxious that it should be on time. The train pulled out, and the passengers settled themselves as best they could for a tedious afternoon ride.

In the smoking room of the rear sleeper sat six traveling men—a shoe man, a shirt man, two grocery men, a hardware man, and a dry-goods man. All were going home for Christmas; with the exception of the dry-goods man, all were married.

The two grocery men, the hardware man, and the dry-goods man started a game of cards. The shirt man opened the daily paper bought at the dinner station. It was all "Christmas," and it made him so homesick that he threw it on the seat and puffed vigorously at his cigar. He had been gone long, and now must miss his Christmas dinner with his wife and babies. One of them he had never seen.

The shoe man was looking out of the window, but his eyes were not on the scenery. He was trying to look into a little home five hundred miles away and see what they were doing for Christmas.

The hardware man puffed away at his cigar for a few minutes and then threw it in the corner. "Don't taste good," he said. He was thinking of home.

With the exception of the dry-goods man, the players weren't thinking of the game, and for fully five minutes at a stretch no one would speak.

* * * * *

In the middle section of the sleeper sat a woman whose voice had thrilled thousands. She was on her way to spend Christmas with friends in one of the cities of Kansas. She must miss the Christmas dinner: the thought made her cross. She found fault with everything and everybody.

Across the aisle from her sat a mother with her little blue-eyed, golden-haired two-year-old beside her. They were on their way to spend Christmas with the "old folks." Her husband, a traveling man, was to meet them there. Now they

would be late. She felt like crying.

The little girl was tired; she "bothered" Mamma. Her mother shook her and set her in the corner of the section, where she cried softly.

The big "compound"* was making the ground tremble with its roar as it dragged the train up the steep grade. The clouds of black smoke rolling back over the train would sometimes shut out the view.

Then the train came to a sudden stop. "What's the matter?" was asked of a brakeman who came through the car.

"Freight got a couple of cars off the track trying to take the switch ahead of us."

"How long will it take to put them on?"

" 'Bout two hours."

This was the last straw—no hope for any eastern connections now.

"Let's take a walk," said the shoe man to the shirt man, and together they started off toward a little clump of cottonwoods about a hundred yards distant, the only trees to be seen for miles. Just within the edge of the little grove they came upon a man standing beside a narrow, gravelike hole he had evidently just dug.

"Prospecting?" asked the shoe man.

He shook his head.

Then they saw that his face bore a sad expression. His eyes looked as though he had been weeping.

"Grave?" asked the shoe man.

He nodded his head.

"For whom?" The tone was one of sympathy.

"My little girl," said the man. After a few moments he

---

* Engine.

went on: "We lived in western Kansas. Our little girl was always sickly. Doctor said, 'Try the mountains,' so we sold out and started in our wagon. But it was too late." His voice broke. "She died last night. It's a long ways to the next town, and we don't know a soul in the Territory, so we concluded we'd bury her here ourselves." And then, looking wistfully at the two men, he asked: "Be either of you men a preacher? Wife can't stand it to bury the little one without someone to make a prayer and sing a song."

* * * * *

Both men felt something rise in their throats. It was the shoe man who spoke. "We are not preachers, but"—he hesitated—"we will see that your baby is buried as a Christian."

"She is over yonder," said the man, pointing to a covered wagon near the other side of the little grove.

"We will be back in a few minutes," said the shoe man, and, taking the shirt man by the arm, he started toward the train. About halfway there he stopped and said, "I've got a Testament in my suitcase; my little girl put it there before I started on this trip. You read a chapter and say a word or two, I'll try to make a prayer, and I'll ask that singer to sing a song. We'll get the other four boys for bearers."

"We can get the boys," answered the other, "but that singer won't move out of her seat."

"You get the boys. I'll ask her anyway." Then he entered the car, walked boldly to her seat, and said, "Pardon me for speaking to you. I'm asking a favor for a mother." In a few words he told the story, and then he asked, "Will you sing something for that mother?"

"Yes," she answered and at once followed him.

The mother across the aisle heard the story. Out of curiosity, perhaps, more than anything else, she followed, carrying the baby in her arms. The six men, the singer, the mother and her baby, followed by perhaps a dozen of the other passengers soon reached the wagon in that little clump of trees.

A long shoebox that had held household goods had been emptied of its contents. A fancy quilt had been folded and placed in the box, covering the bottom and sides, and on this, her little head resting on a small pillow, was his little girl—a sweet-faced child of perhaps five years. Folded in her arms was a battered doll. By the side of the rough box knelt the mother. She had gathered an apronful of the bright-colored dead leaves. These she was arranging around the inside of the box, and she was talking to that still form as though it yet could hear and understand.

Her husband touched her arm. "Mary," said he, "here are some folks to help us."

She rose to her feet. "I knew God would send someone," she answered simply.

The shirt man stepped to the foot and the shoe man to the head of that rough little coffin. The shirt man remembered a chapter he had often heard read and had found it in the little Testament. "Let not your heart be troubled. In my Father's house are many mansions. I go to prepare a place for you," he read. Then the shoe man prayed that though the grave was far from any human dwelling, the angels would mark the spot till Jesus returned.

The two grocery men, the hardware man, and the dry-goods man carried the rough little coffin to the grave and lowered it with a couple of picket ropes while the shoe man said: "Earth to earth; ashes to ashes; and dust to dust."

At this point the singer, clasping her hands and raising her eyes toward heaven, sang with all the sweetness and tenderness of her marvelous voice of heaven's love and care. Then stepping to the mother's side, she said, "Come," and gently led her back to her wagon.

In a few minutes the men filled the grave and made a mound of stones over it; then they walked back to the wagon with the father. But the singer and the mother sat together on a box, their arms around each other, and there were tears on both faces.

* * * * *

A whistle sounded. The singer kissed the mother. The husband pressed the hand of each of the six men and said simply, "Gentlemen, you are all strangers, but you have been kind to us in our trouble, and we thank you."

Glancing back after he had gone a few yards, the shoe man saw the wife with her arms around her husband's neck and heard her say, "Wasn't God good to send someone to pray and sing for baby?"

The train sped on, but the game of cards was not finished. The little golden-haired tot did not "bother" Mamma anymore, but was held close and heard stories until the short winter afternoon drew to a close. A baby song, and the little one was fast asleep—laid upon the seat and covered with a wrap.

The singer spoke pleasantly to the white-haired old lady in the seat in front of her. A mother with three little ones occupied a section near the front of the car. As it grew dark, the little ones became fretful and restless. The singer walked to the front of the car, took the youngest in her arms and sang a baby song, and the tired little head dropped on her shoulder fast asleep. Still holding the little one in her arms, she told the others wonderful Christmas stories until interrupted by the brakeman calling: "Thirty minutes for supper. Passengers for the South will change cars."

William McGinnies wrote for magazines during the first half of the twentieth century.

Joy to the World

Mary Russell

Elaine Spencer was the only student left in the dormitory, three thousand miles from home. How she longed to be home for Christmas.

But one thing was certain: she must escape this empty building.

So she put on her coat, and shut the door.

* * * * *

Elaine Spencer rose from her chair and stood in the center of the room, listening. But no familiar sounds came to her. No voice called from one room to another. No hurrying feet rushed over the stairs. No singer crooned from the radio. No telephone rang.

Well, she hadn't expected they would. Students Hall was deserted, its girls gone for the holidays. Elaine had planned to be home by this time, to be with her family in California. Instead she was here in Boston, alone in the huge, empty Hall.

Last year, it hadn't been so bad. She had known that she couldn't return home for Christmas. That had been decided before she left home. The fare from one coast to the other was too high for frequent trips, so she had agreed to remain in the East until the second Christmas. That first year she had gone home with one of the girls and enjoyed all the thrills of

a New England holiday season: coasting, skiing, skating, and customs unlike any she had known in the warm Southland.

But this year it was different. Her mother's letter had come abruptly, telling of the need for special economy, and suggesting that the price of her ticket be saved and applied on her expenses at the conservatory.

Elaine had agreed. She would make any sacrifice to go on with her music. But that didn't ease the loneliness or make it pleasant to be alone in a strange city on Christmas Eve.

She crossed to the window and looked out on the snow-covered streets, the darkness, the hurrying pedestrians, the swiftly moving cars. She shivered. How different from the palm-bordered street on which her home stood. Why, the poinsettias would be blooming against the house, and the shrubs would be loaded with red berries, the air warm and balmy! But here in Boston it was cold, drear, lonely.

She had told none of her schoolmates of the change in her plans. For weeks she had been telling of her coming trip home, of the exciting times awaiting her, and had listened to the half-envious exclamations of her friends. She couldn't tell them that her dream had burst; she couldn't accept their well-meant sympathy or their hastily proffered invitations. So she had kept silent about her disappointment and had said goodbye with a smile.

But when the last girl had gone, when she was alone in that silent room, Elaine had tasted the bitterness of disappointment and known the crushing agony of homesickness.

Now her restless fingers tapped the frosted pane. What should she do? She couldn't stay alone all evening in that great silent building with its shadows and memories. But where should she go? Outside her student circle she had no

friends in the city. She had no shopping to be done—her gifts were already sent. But she must get out, go somewhere.

Quickly she combed her hair and pulled her gray felt hat down over it. Then she slipped into her warm coat, picked up gloves and purse, and left the room. Down the wide stairs and past darkened rooms she went. Only the caretaker and his wife shared the house with her, and they were in the rear, not even knowing that she was there.

She opened the door and stepped out into the night. Clear, cold, crisp—a perfect Christmas Eve for New England. But Elaine didn't know that. She saw no significance in the bright stars that shone so clear and steady; no beauty in the snow that covered the ground like a white blanket. She didn't hear the music of the crunching snow under her feet. She felt only the cold, and responded by turning her collar higher, thrusting her hands into her pockets, and walking faster.

The subway was crowded. Elaine had to stand and cling to a strap, jostled and pushed by the moving crowd. No one noticed her. Why should they? She meant nothing to them. She shut her lips tightly and lifted her head higher.

At the Common she left the train, glad to escape from the packed car. The park lay white and glistening, its leafless trees making quaint shadows on the snowy areas between walks, but Elaine didn't see this. For an instant she let her attention wander to the huge tree that stood there with its burden of colored lights. She had read in the paper that the tree had been constructed of hundreds of small trees brought from the north woods. So perfect was the work that no trace of its manufacture was evident. It stood there, a magnificent Christmas tree, greeting all who passed.

Elaine's thoughts flew to her native city in Southern California. There lawns would be alight with decorated living trees. Even shrubs about doors would hold their quota of shining bulbs. On this Christmas Eve, while she stood alone in a cold park, her family and friends would be driving along the streets, admiring the lighted trees.

Presently Elaine became conscious of hurrying crowds of people passing her, all going in one direction. Men, women, children, and young people were leaving the shops and the town. Hardly knowing that she did so, she joined the moving throng. Across the Common, up narrow streets to old historic Beacon Hill, from every side street came more people, until the hill was literally covered. Not a car or truck was in sight. What could it mean?

Then Elaine noticed the houses. Every one of them was ablaze with lights. Shades were up, curtains drawn back, and candles twinkled in the windows. Candles everywhere! In some homes there was a candle for every small windowpane; in others, rows and rows, one above another.

Suddenly, Elaine lifted her head and listened. The sound of carols reached her ear, faintly, coming from afar. Suddenly, a group directly in front of her joined the carolers, and "Joy to the World" rang out on the cold winter night. Others took up the refrain until the air was full of music. Elaine responded to the inspiring demonstration.

Then "The First Noel" rose clear and sweet. Something stirred within Elaine. Hardly knowing that she did so, she began to hum the air softly. She joined the second stanza with the words. Her clear, trained voice took the high notes and added to the volume. A young tenor beside her gave her an admiring glance, and as the carol ended, he smiled, and Elaine smiled in return.

When the group started to move on, the young man said, "Better go the rest of the way with us. You're a splendid addition." And Elaine went.

Another stop and they came to a hospital. A nurse greeted them from the lighted doorway. "They are waiting," she said with a smile. The group of carolers entered, stood within the wide hallway at the foot of the stairs, and sent their voices echoing down the corridors.

Elaine had sung in church, at school, on concert programs, but always before an audience. Here was an audience, but unseen. Who composed it? Men, women, children, young people? None of them could go home for Christmas. She must sing for them. No one must miss the carols. She lifted her voice and sang with definite purpose, forgetting herself, her disappointment, her loneliness. She thought only of those others, so in need of cheer and hope.

Then they were in front of an old brownstone home. A

sweet-faced woman with snow-white hair stood in the open doorway bidding them enter.

"We always end here," Elaine's escort explained. "She serves us refreshments."

"But I mustn't go in with you," Elaine protested.

"Sure you do," the young man answered. "Anyone who helps with the caroling is welcome. You've come this far," he said with a laugh, "better go the rest of the way."

A yule log burned slowly in the wide fireplace. The soft golden glow from candles filtered through the spacious rooms. Sweet fragrance of evergreens scented the air, while smiling women served refreshments, and the genial hostess presented each caroler with a tiny package wrapped in Christmas paper and silver ribbon.

"You should be in our choir."

Elaine turned at her companion's words.

"But I don't live here," she answered. "I'm only here for study. At home I'm in the choir, but here—"

"What's the matter with here?" asked the young man. "Just as many weekends as there are back home. Only they're much longer and lonelier when you don't know anyone."

"Oh, I know," Elaine answered, though for a time she had forgotten.

"My home is in Kansas. The first year I was at Harvard I was horribly lonesome and—well, yes, homesick. Then I joined this choir, and now I feel I belong." He turned to smile at her.

Elaine told him of her work at the conservatory and of her home in California. Suddenly, she was telling him of her changed plans, her disappointment, her aimless following of the crowd. She hadn't meant to tell so much, but once started, the words came. As she talked, she smiled. She was still missing her family, but she wasn't as lonely as an hour earlier, not crushed by self-pity. She sensed her companion's understanding.

Then they were going down the hill together. At the entrance to the subway, he asked, "Why don't you have Christmas dinner with me tomorrow? We can help each other to be less lonely." And she agreed.

The subway was crowded. Elaine couldn't find a seat, but she didn't care. She didn't even mind when a woman with a large bulky parcel jostled against her. Everyone seemed to have parcels. She almost wished she had one.

She must have smiled at the thought, for a man standing near smiled at her and exhibited the partially wrapped tricycle he was carrying. "It's for my little grandson," he said. He seemed to think that Elaine would be interested, and she was.

A woman sitting in front of Elaine had a long narrow box on her knees. Anyone would know it contained a doll. It made Elaine think of her own little sister. She smiled at the woman, and the woman smiled back. Everyone seemed to be ready with smiles.

An old lady broke a bit of green from her tiny Christmas tree and held it toward Elaine. "Here, dear, pin it on your coat. Everybody should wear a bit of Christmas green. Most of them have holly, but fir is just as good."

"Better," Elaine said. She was smelling again the fragrance of that home on Beacon Hill and feeling its Christmas cheer.

On the street again she paused, inhaled deeply, looked about. What a wonderful night! Glistening snow, starry heavens, decorated homes—Christmas Eve!

With quickened steps she covered the half-block to the

Hall, unlocked the door, and ran lightly upstairs to her room. A holly wreath gleamed on her door, a poinsettia ornamented her desk, a package lay on her couch. The caretaker and his wife must have discovered that she was still there.

As she made ready for the night, she hummed softly, "Joy to the world! The Lord is come."

Suddenly she stopped, held by the thought that had flashed into her mind. It was because He came that she was no longer lonely though alone, that she had found friends among strangers, that she would have dinner with one of them tomorrow, that she might join a church choir, that she had helped to cheer others. Why, all she valued most in life was the result of His coming, and because His Spirit remained in the world! Of course, she had always known that in a way, but she had never really appreciated its significance before.

She slowly crossed to the window, threw it open, and gazed up at the heavens. Their glory filled her with joy. She would never forget this Christmas. In the years to come, whether in California or Boston, she would remember and be glad, for it had brought her this priceless gift—an understanding of Christmas.

The words of her new friend came to her again, but with a different meaning. "You've come this far. Better go the rest of the way." She would go the rest of the way to help others make the discovery that she had, to realize what His coming meant to them and to the world. She closed the window softly, her eyes alight with joy.

Mary Russell wrote for magazines during the first half of the twentieth century.

The Lighted Path

Temple Bailey

Every woman wants to be loved and needed. But after courtship, after marriage, after children, after responsibility—what if the magical love that started everything fades in the reality of practical things?

* * * * *

"Take a lantern," the Mother said.

"We need no light. There is a moon."

But the Mother insisted—"The moon is not enough."

So the children went away, swinging the lantern.

The path they followed led through a wood. It was a pine wood; and the trees were close together, their branches making a roof which shut out the moonlight. But the moon was not shut out on the path, which was a silver thread in the tapestry of the night.

The children were not afraid of the dark wood, for they had often gone that way. They sang as they went, and the Girl's voice was a treble chime, and the Boy's like a deep-toned bell. It was very cold, and their voices carried far. There was not a cloud in the sky, nor a sign of snow on the pine needles. And it was Christmas Eve.

At the edge of the wood they met their Father. "Mother made us bring a lantern."

And their Father said, "She would, of course." He lifted the lantern and blew out the light. "The moon is enough," he said.

Then the Boy said, "Which shall we believe? Our Mother says the moon is not enough. You say that it is. Shall we believe you or our Mother?"

The Father stood for a moment looking up at the bright moon. "You must think that out for yourselves," he replied. "Perhaps I see more light than there is; perhaps your Mother sees less. I look up at the sky. She looks down at the path. She may be right. I may be right. Who knows?"

And the Girl said, "I like looking up at the sky."

But the Boy considered it. "When the path is rough, we need a lantern."

And the Father laughed and said, "We'll have light enough in the town. And we are going to buy a Christmas present for your Mother."

They were on the road now, which was broad and smooth; and stretching up on each side of it were great farms, with their barns and houses making sharp shadows on the hills; and after a while the farms gave way to rows of cottages; and at last the Father and the children came to the village street, with shops on each side and with crowds surging back and forth and up and down.

And the windows of the shops were gay with their multi-colored wares; and in the market shops were turkeys ready for roasting, and plumes of celery, and cranberries red as rubies, and oranges and a few choice strawberries in a green basket. And in the crockery shop were dinner sets and painted vases and pots and pans; and on the top shelf a bowl of amber glass which seemed to melt into sunshine as the light shone upon

it. And in the dress shop were gowns and hats and coats and furs, and a white scarf woven with a golden thread. And at the florist's were holly and mistletoe and evergreen wreaths; and set somewhat back in a corner a tight little bunch of saffron roses.

And the children, walking slowly with their Father in front of the shops, asked, "What will you get for Mother?"

And the Father said, "What do you think?"

And the Boy said, "She needs a new coat."

And the Girl said, "She needs pots and pans."

And the Father said, "Do you know what I would buy if I had my way? I would buy the amber bowl and the saffron roses and the white scarf with the gold thread and the strawberries in the green basket."

And the children looked at him with startled eyes; and the Boy said, "What would she do with roses and a golden scarf?"

"She would wear the roses at her breast and the scarf about her white neck as she once wore them."

And the Girl said, "Why doesn't she wear them now?"

"She has forgotten romance," the Father said; and there was a touch of bitterness in his voice. "And romance to me is food and drink."

He turned away quickly from the florist's window and went with the children down the street and bought a warm coat and an iron pot and four pans.

And when they came again to the edge of the wood, the Girl asked, "Shall we light the lantern?"

And the Father said, "No, we have the moon."

So the children went on in the moonlight, singing, and the Father sang with them; and when he had sung for a time he stopped and said, "I used to sing to your Mother."

"Why don't you sing to her now?"

"She cares no more for singing."

They walked in silence after that; and all at once the Girl stumbled.

"I couldn't see the path," she sobbed. And the Boy said, "We'd better light the lantern."

So they came to the house with the lantern lighted, and the Mother met them at the door. "You're late," she said, "and the supper's spoiling."

So the four of them sat down at the table. It was a square table with a white cloth and a dish of red apples in the center. And the food was wonderful: crusty bread and sweet, fresh butter and eggs like daffodils on a blue platter and squares of honey in small glass saucers and a great pitcher of milk with the cream on it.

And the Mother took her seat at the table and poured a hot drink for the Father and milk for the children.

And the Girl, eating her egg and drinking her milk, wondered how her Mother would look with a golden scarf about her neck and a rose at her breast.

But her Mother was saying, "We must all help with the dishes, and then the children must go to bed."

And the Boy and Girl knew why they must go to bed. It was because it was Christmas Eve; and there was a tree to be trimmed by their Father and Mother.

So the Mother scraped the plates and carried them to the kitchen, and had hot suds in one shining pan and hot clear water in another, and the children wiped the china on clean, checked towels, and while they wiped they told the Mother of the things they had seen in town.

"We saw strawberries," said the Boy, "in a green basket."

"And a golden scarf."

"And an amber bowl."

"And little yellow roses."

"And Father said you used to wear them."

And as they said these things, the Mother's hands were still—and at last the Boy said, "Are you thinking of the roses, Mother?"

And the Mother said, "Why should I think of roses?"

And she went to work with a will; and presently she dried her hands and said, "I'll stir up the buckwheat cakes for tomorrow's breakfast, and then everything will be finished."

But the Boy and Girl knew that everything would not be finished, for there was yet the Tree.

When they went upstairs, the moon was still shining, and as the children stood looking out the hall window toward the east, the Girl said, "At midnight the angels will be singing."

And the Boy said, "The animals will be kneeling."

The Girl said, "Do you believe it?"

And the Boy said, "Mother believes it."

And the Girl said, "If Mother believes it, it is true."

Then the Boy went to his room and to sleep; but the Girl lay long awake, thinking of the things that had happened. And most of

all she thought of how her Mother had told her to take the lantern, and how her Father had blown it out. Yet without the lantern, she had stumbled.

And downstairs the Father went into the wood and brought in the tree he had cut, and the Mother brought a box of glittering balls and tinsel chains, and a great pan of corn that she popped; and the Father flung the tinsel over the branches of the tree, and tied on the golden balls, and as he worked he whistled a rollicking tune. And his wife said as she strung the popcorn, "You are always like a boy at Christmas."

And the Father laughed, and said in his eager voice, "I love it all, the holly and the mistletoe, and the color and the carols. I love the poetry of it, and the old traditions."

The Mother's voice had

a touch of wistfulness. "I love that too; but best of all I love the thought of the angels singing—"

And the Father said, "That's part of the poetry."

And the Mother shook her head. "It's more than that."

But she did not pursue the thought, for the popcorn chains were ready. And as they hung the chains over the branches, the Father and Mother came closer and closer until at last they met. And the Father, bending down to the Mother's flushed cheek, kissed it.

And she flushed more than ever and said, "Love me?"

And he said, "Yes."

And after that they hung the children's presents on the tree; and the things the Mother had bought were warm and practical, like stockings and gloves and handkerchiefs; and the things the Father had bought were silly things that wound up with a key, so that the donkeys kicked and the clowns danced and the mice ran under your feet. And there was a blue fan for the Girl; and for the Boy a book of verses.

When she saw the fan, the Mother said, with a note of sharpness, "Weren't you being a bit extravagant?"

And the Father said, with coldness, "If you choose to call it that."

The Mother said, "I'm sorry. But the children need so many things."

And the Father said, "Beauty is food for the soul."

And after that he did not whistle; and presently they went to bed.

And in the morning the Mother got up early to bake the buckwheat cakes. When the children came in, she kissed them and said, "A merry Christmas, darlings."

And they kissed her and said, "A merry Christmas."

And the Mother took from a shelf a worn, black book, and said, "While we wait for Father shall we read a chapter?"

So they read of the Wise Men and the Babe in the Manger, and the Mother said, "He was a wonderful Child. I want you to be like Him."

And the children said, "You are like Mary, Mother."

And suddenly they saw her face grow stern. "No," she said, "I am not like Mary. I am like that other woman in the Bible—Martha."

And then she got up and began to bake the buckwheat cakes.

And when the Father came down, there was a smell of sausage frying; and on the table was a jug of translucent syrup, and when the buckwheat cakes came on, they were brown as berries and as light as feathers.

And the Father said to the children, "Do you know you have a marvelous Mother?"

And they said, "She says she's not like Mary—she's like Martha."

And the Father looked up at his wife and asked, "What made you say that?"

And she said, "Because it is true."

And after breakfast they had their presents; and the children looked at the stockings and gloves and the nice handkerchiefs that their Mother had bought, and they thanked their Mother and kissed her, and then they laid aside the things she had given them and played with their toys and shouted with laughter, and their Father played with them.

Then they brought out the presents for their Mother, and she untied the strings and undid the papers and found the warm coat and the pot and the four tin pans. And the Girl

watching her face asked anxiously, "Don't you like them?"

And she smiled and said, "Indeed I do, my darling." And she rolled up the string carefully and folded the rest of the wrappings and carried them all out to the kitchen.

And after that she was very busy getting ready for the Christmas dinner. There were to be guests—two uncles and two aunts and a lot of cousins; and there was the turkey to be roasted and the giblets to be chopped and the turnips to be peeled and the potatoes, and the pudding to be watched.

And when the guests arrived and sat down, there were seven of them; and one was a young cousin who had just been married. And her hair was waved and her eyes shining, and she showed them a little golden heart that her young husband had given her.

"He really couldn't afford it," she said, with a sort of splendid rapture, "but I love him for it."

And there flashed between her and her young husband a look that drove the blood from the cheeks of the Mother of the children. For there had been a time when her own young husband had looked at her like that.

But she set her mind resolutely not to think of it; and presently she and the children cleared the table, and the pudding was brought in and the tree was lighted and the popcorn looked like snow.

And the youngest of the uncles said, "We should have had a snowy Christmas. Nothing is as it used to be."

Suddenly, the Mother of the children spoke, "Does anyone think in these days of the Babe in the Manger?"

And the oldest uncle, who had white hair and a wise heart, said, "There is more kindness and peace in the world than ever before. And if that is so, the Babe is among us."

And silence fell upon them at the thought that the Babe was there.

And after dinner the Father of the children took them for a walk, and when the children came back they were alone. And their Mother asked, "Where is your Father?"

They said, "He went into town."

And the Mother of the children moved about the room putting everything in order; and when she had finished, she opened the door and looked out. Night had come on and the moon was shining, so that the whole world was white with radiance. And the Mother of the children walked down the silver path to meet her husband. She had wrapped herself in the warm coat and the strong wind which blew from the north buffeted her. At last she came to the edge of the wood, and looked down the broad road and saw no sign of her husband. For a moment she was afraid; but as she turned her face up to the shining sky, her heart was stilled. For it seemed to her that in a world of such beauty there could be no place for doubt or despair.

Presently she turned back; and now the north wind blew with increasing violence, and the sky was clouded, so when she came to the house she got the lantern and set it on the steps to light the way for her husband.

And the Mother went to the foot of the stairs and called up to the children, "It is time for bed," and they asked, "Has Father come?" She said, "No, but I shall wait for him."

So she sat by the fire and waited. And the flames of the fire shone on her, and she was transfigured. But she was afraid to look at the clock it was so late; and it was not until she counted eleven strokes that her husband came. He crossed the room and knelt beside her and his cheek was cold against

her cheek. And he said, "My dear and my darling."

And she looked into his eyes and said, "Do you think of me like that?"

And he said, "You know I do."

And she said, "I have not always known it," and her voice faltered.

He drew her close. "Listen," he said, "and I will tell you: Last night I went into town with the children. And my heart was bitter because I was tired of a world that was all work and weariness. And I wanted to be gay and young, and I wanted you to be young, with your hair loose and flowers at your breast. And because I was bitter, I blamed you for what life had brought us, and I made the children blow out the lantern and said that the moon was enough. And we came to the town and I wanted roses for you and a golden scarf—but I bought you a coat and a pot and pans because I thought you had forgotten."

Against his heart she murmured, "I had not forgotten."

He went on. "Then we came home through the dark wood, and we walked again without the lantern, and one of the children stumbled and was hurt, and all at once I knew you were right when you said they needed more light on the path than the moon gave them. And last night I lay awake and thought of it all—of how you had flushed when I kissed you on the cheek, and of how you had sacrificed youth and girlish vanity for the sake of the children. And of how you had kept our little house clean and shining. And when I saw you today sitting at our table, serene and smiling and thinking not of yourself but of the happiness of others, I knew that even the young bride was not more beautiful. For there is a loveliness in women which men go mad about; but there is also a loveliness which they adore—the Mother of the home is an angel."

She stirred in his arms. "Am I just the Mother of a home?"

He smiled at her. "You are my dear and my darling. When I came tonight to the edge of the dark wood, there, constant as a star, was the light you had set for me. You are that to me—my star—"

Her cheek was wet as he laid his own against it. And presently he said, "Do you know why I stayed so late?"

And she said, "No."

And he said, "I wanted you to have your roses. And there were none left in the shop where I had seen them, so I went on to the next town; and by luck I found them."

He left her for a moment and came back with the roses in his hand. And the Mother put one of them against her lips and against his lips; and when she laughed, her laugh was like a song.

"I love my pots and pans," she said, "because you have made them beautiful; and I love my warm coat, because when I wear it your arms are about me; and I love the lantern and the moon, because the moon gives a light which is like the love of God, and the lantern is the love we have for each other—and we shall need them both as we walk the path together . . ."

———————————

Temple Bailey was born in Petersburg, Virginia, and became one of America's most popular—and highest paid—authors.

Let Nothing You Dismay

Ruth P. Harnden

Oh my! She was getting so forgetful! Now she had an awful feeling in the pit of her stomach that she'd botched up things again: sent the wrong—the very wrong—packages to two people she loved very much.

* * * * *

For twenty-two long years this story has been staring accusingly in my face: Why don't you love me like you do all those others? And for twenty-two years Christmas-loving readers have kept sending me copies, urging me to include it in a collection. So, I give up. Its time has come.

* * * * *

She had spent the afternoon trimming the tree. She had trimmed it after the fashion of her native land, with bright red polished apples hanging, for balance and for beauty, under each pure-white candle. The old customs and her distant youth were sharp to her memory. Sometimes they were sharper than the events of her present life in this New England village where she had come so many years ago and raised her American family. Sometimes, and more often of late, she would find herself forgetting things that had happened only the week before. She would make confusing mistakes, answer letters she had answered already, or else forget to answer them at all. It surprised her very much. She could remember so brilliantly every tree in her mother's garden, every street in the small Swedish town where she had grown up, the faces and names of her early playmates and neighbors. It was very puzzling.

She sat now in the dark room, in the fragrance from the balsam tree, and watched the year's first snow falling beyond the window. She wouldn't light the candles yet. She was saving them for the children. If the snow kept up, she knew, it would make the walking bad. But she hoped that it would keep up. She found it beautiful—and more than that. She had never lost, or perhaps she had found again, a childlike sense of magic in the presence of the first snowfall.

How strange it must be, she thought, *to live where there is always snow.* There was Hilda in the mountains of Oregon—Hilda who had cooked for her so faithfully until she married that crazy miner and went to live in some shack in the wilds. So *cold,* she would write in her letters. *Always so cold it is. I think I never be warm again.*

Rocking gently in the warm room, smelling the Christmas tree, watching the quick, feathered air outside, she thought with satisfaction of the socks she had knit for Hilda. Six pairs, extra heavy. Hilda's feet, at least, would be warm.

She had mailed them in plenty of time. Last week, wasn't it? And there was still a week to go before Christmas. But then, she asked herself abruptly, what was it that she had mailed this morning? Something to Hilda, she was sure. She remembered thinking of her at the post office this morning, and she had written on the wide, flat box . . . But that was impossible! That was the nightie for Janie, who was getting married right after Christmas.

Her granddaughter getting married! Only think. It was hard to realize. And it was the loveliest nightie she could find, the color of honeysuckle and trimmed with real lace. "Extravagant," she told herself dutifully now, but it didn't prevent her from smiling. It was so beautiful, and so was Janie—and she was getting married. Nineteen. Janie was nineteen. It didn't seem possible. And she had sent the nightie this morning to . . .

JAMES MONTGOMERY FLAGG

She stopped the gently rocking chair and sat straighter, trying to stop her thoughts until she could straighten them.

She had stood at the table in the post office, under the placard listing the states and their mailing dates—"For Florida," "For Oregon"—and she had thought of Hilda. "Oh, dear!" she said aloud, because now she could remember very clearly writing Mrs. Hilda Borge, writing the Oregon address. "And the socks?" she asked herself. Had she sent the socks to Janie in Florida? But she could write to Janie. She could explain. It was of Hilda that she needed to think.

For a moment she was seeing the plain and practical Hilda with an awful clarity, because she was seeing her in relation to the bridal nightie, the gleaming satin, the cobweb lace. It was a picture so incongruous as to be almost indecent. And no one would be quicker to know that than Hilda herself. How she scorned all softness, all luxury and beauty, out of the protective shell she had built around her own poverty and plainness. "Such nonsense," she could hear Hilda saying, "when so many are hungry and cold." But it was really the beauty that Hilda feared, as though she had to deny its existence or she would have to admit her own deprivation—her small, middle-aged, shapeless body; her homely, work-scarred hands; the hopeless plainness of her face. She was unredeemed by a single beauty, and it was a wonder that anyone—even the thickheaded, bowlegged miner—had wanted to marry her.

Would Hilda ever understand that her sending that exquisite gossamer nightie into her poor, stark shack where, in all likelihood, she slept in her long woolen underwear was only an old woman's fumbling mistake and not an insult, not a mockery? Or would it break her heart with its terrible contrast to her own ugliness; its terrible reminder of all the luxury and loveliness that had no place in her life?

How could I? she asked herself. *And for Christmas too?* The happiest time of the year. The time for remembering old friends with love and with loving gifts. Even now in the distance, but still distinctly, she could hear the carol singers lifting their voices on the sharp and snow-filled air. "God rest you merry, gentlemen, let nothing you dismay . . ." How ironic the words seemed to her now, like a rebuke to her shameful stupidity, her cruel blunder.

It was only the day after Christmas that she had Janie's wire from Miami—Janie who was so young and impatient, and too busy with her wedding plans to sit down and write a letter. *Marvelous ski socks,* the wire read. *How did you guess where we were spending our honeymoon?*

So that, at least, was all right, even though she had forgotten to write an explanation to Janie. Now she was glad that she hadn't written. Ski socks, indeed! It made her think of her own youth in Sweden, and it was several minutes before her mind returned to the present. But that meant that she *had* sent the nightie to Hilda! For a little while, for a few happy Christmas days, she had forgotten.

It was another week before Hilda's letter came. *Old Hilda,* it began—in the middle of her own thought, after the habit of her simplicity. For a second she thought her worst fears had been realized, and her heart shook. But her eyes moved rapidly on. *Old Hilda, they think, there is only to keep her warm. So they send the sweaters, the mittens, the socks. What could make her pretty, such a one, eh? But you, my lovely friend, you have the other heart, the other eyes, and I am beautiful now! I open up the tight-air stove so the room is full of heat, and I put on my beautiful dress made for dancing, and what you think? I dance! Old Hilda*

dances, can you think of it? And my Tim he come and dance with
me. Ha! I think my Tim he fall in love with me all over again.

Ruth P. Harnden wrote during the first half of the twentieth century.

A Warmth in Her Heart

Goldie Down

The bottom fell out of the tired nurse's life when a thief smashed in the back window of her car just to get to the Christmas presents she and the other nurses had sacrificed to buy and wrap for their patients! She could only weep.

But then—

* * * * *

O h, no! How could anyone be so mean? Tears stung Glenda's eyes as she stared at the empty car seat. A smashed rear window told what had happened. Some thief had seen the carton of gift-wrapped packages and made off with it.

He must have known those packages were intended for the patients. Glenda's hand shook as she tried to insert the ignition key. The lettering on the car door was large enough for anyone to read: DISTRICT HEALTH SERVICE.

All the way to the nursing depot Glenda alternated between sobbing and seething. Today was Christmas Eve, and she had planned to distribute the gifts as she made her rounds. Now the packages were gone. What could she say to her patients? Poor darlings, most of them had so little joy.

It wasn't fair! Glenda bit her lower lip to still its trembling. Her thoughts flew back to the previous afternoon when the nurses had handed in their reports and received their pay. With one accord, they had cheerfully chipped in and purchased choice fruit and other goodies for their patients. Then they had stayed behind and on their own time and filled the little baskets, covering them with gleaming red cellophane and tying them with green ribbons. The sprig of holly taped on top of each had been Glenda's idea. It made the gift baskets look so Christmasy. Each nurse had counted her patients and taken the number of baskets she required and packed them into her work car.

And now Glenda's baskets had been stolen. "It's not fair!" she burst out, her eyes skimmed over the pushing, hurrying, heedless crowds thronging the sidewalk. *You selfish people! What do you care about the old and sick and lonely? I hate the lot of you!* She jammed on the brakes and lurched to a stop in front of the nursing depot.

"Not really!" "Stealing Christmas gifts?" "Where's all the goodwill?" The other nurses gathered around, listening to Glenda's story and commiserating with her, but there was nothing they could do. It was too late to buy more fruit and package it; patients were waiting for baths and treatments. One by one the nurses revved up their cars and left to do their rounds. With a heavy heart and an empty car, Glenda followed them.

* * * * *

Left alone in the silent office, Adrienne, the supervisor,

sat at her desk deep in thought. Something ought to be done. Such caddish behavior, particularly at Christmastime, ought to be publicized. Maybe the thief would feel ashamed.

I'll tell the newspaper, she thought, impulsively reaching for the telephone and dialing the city's largest daily.

After word-pushing her way past a battery of secretaries, Adrienne finally heard the editor's smooth voice ask, "What can I do for you?"

"I'm one of the district nurses in the inner city," Adrienne said. "Yesterday we paid out of our own salaries for Christmas baskets for our patients. Most of them live alone— old-age pensioners, very poor and lonely. Now some of the gifts are gone. A thief smashed the car window—" Words and sentences jumbled together

as Adrienne breathlessly poured her story into the distant ear.

"Hmm." The smooth voice paused, then came again. "Tomorrow is Christmas Day. It will be too late to do anything by the time your story is printed in the morning paper. Why don't you phone the radio? There's a phone-in talk show in about half an hour. You could phone and tell your story. Wait, I'll give you the number."

"Thank you!" Adrienne said, gulping. Her thoughts whirled as she jotted down the number and replaced the receiver. Oh dear, should she have started this? Where would it lead? What could she say on the air?

Well, she might as well go through with it now. With trembling haste she dialed the radio station and told her story again. The voice at the other end said,

"Right, we'll put you on. Hold the line."

Too late now to change her mind! Almost before she realized it, she was telling her story for the third time, and now radio waves were carrying it the length and breadth of the city.

When she finished, the lady *compère's** silky voice asked, "And what now, Adrienne? What do you want done about this?"

Adrienne almost dropped the telephone. She hadn't thought of this! In her grief and anger she had thought only to advertise the unknown thief's mean behavior. It hadn't occurred to her that anyone could do anything about it.

"I don't know," she faltered into the mouthpiece. "Maybe—perhaps the thief might bring the baskets of fruit back."

A moment's silence and then: "I can think of something better than that," a studio announcer broke in. "Why don't we ask whether any of our listeners would like to demonstrate their Christmas spirit by providing fruit for these patients? How about it, all you happy people out there?"

* * * * *

While all this was going on, Glenda was sadly driving from house to house, tending her patients, and telling her sad story: "I'm sorry, Mr. Moffit," Glenda said as she rubbed alcohol on his arm where she had just given him a shot. "I had a Christmas present for you, but somebody stole it."

"I'm so sorry, Mrs. Smith." She renewed the dressing on the old lady's ulcerated leg. "My Christmas gift to you was stolen."

---

* Radio hostess or master of ceremonies.

"I'm sorry, Gran," she bellowed into the deaf old paralytic's ear as she lifted her out of the bathtub. "I had a Christmas gift wrapped and ready to bring you, but—"

Worn out physically and emotionally, Glenda completed her rounds and drove back to the nursing depot. An excited young secretary met her at the door.

"Oh, Glenda, you've got to see all the fruit and stuff!" she exclaimed. "Peaches and cherries! And one man brought two dozen candy bars! And—oh, here's another boxful just come in!" She dashed to the back door.

Mystified, Glenda followed her into the nursing office. The room looked like a fruit market. Baskets of oranges and boxes of plums shared the main desk; a bag of bananas and three pineapples occupied the armchairs; a carton of apricots elbowed the wastebasket. A radiant Adrienne sat with a pile of empty baskets on her lap and the telephone pressed to her ear.

"Oh, thank you," she said. "We'll bring the stuff right over." She put down the phone and beamed at Glenda. "The secretaries at headquarters have heard about all this. They said they're not very busy today, so if we send it all over, they'll package it for us. The red cellophane and ribbon will be their contribution. They've already sent a girl out to buy it."

"But what has happened?" Glenda's eyes widened as the secretary walked in with yet another tray of peaches. "Where has all this fruit come from?"

"I telephoned the newspaper, and the editor directed me to the radio." Adrienne told the story, and as Glenda listened, the ice in her heart melted and tears of joy shone in her brown eyes.

"Some people gave money too." Adrienne pointed to a

pile of coins and paper money on her desk. "Maybe later on we can hire a bus and take some of the mobile patients on an outing somewhere."

Glenda nodded wordlessly.

* * * * *

Two hours later, Glenda was once more steering her car through people-thronged streets, repeating her usual rounds; but this time her heart was warm. The car's backseat was piled with gaily wrapped baskets bigger than the district nurses could have afforded.

"I apologize," she said as she nodded to the pushing, hurrying, heedless crowds. "You've proved that humanity isn't all bad. The Christmas spirit of loving and sharing isn't dead after all."

Goldie Down writes today from her home in Australia.

The Lost Child

Retold by Mabel Lee Cooper

Some stories refuse to die—even after hundreds, even thousands of years. This Christmas story is one of them. A powerful lord had everything he could wish for—everything but inner peace.

So . . . should he let his children make the search?

* * * * *

On the side of a high mountain near the city of Rome stood a wonderful castle. The highland road crossed the mountain in front of the castle and wound by its gate. Above the castle, the tall, stately pine trees rose in a dark background, and below, the forests stretched down to the busy towns in the lowlands. Inside the castle dwelt a good knight with his wife and two children, Felice and Rudolph, and their many servants. They were a happy family—all but the knight. He had an enemy who had greatly wronged him and whom he hated bitterly. His heart being so full of hatred, it seemed that nothing could make him happy or give him peace.

One Christmas night the lights in the castle blazed high, the gate stood open, and a smiling servant bade all who passed to enter in Christ's name. Many wayfarers entered, for a great feast was being held within the castle.

The guests were bidden to enter in Christ's name, but that name was new in that part of the country, for the people who lived there still called on the names of false gods. It happened, however, that about a year before, the knight of this castle had journeyed to the city of Rome. As he strolled along the street, enjoying the noise, gaiety, and color of the great city, he noticed a man in a simple brown coat talking to an ever-increasing crowd. The man was telling of Christ, who had come to earth to teach men a new way of life. The knight drew close to the teacher and said that he would like to know more of The Way of which he was preaching.

The speaker looked kindly upon the knight and asked where he lodged. That evening he came to see the knight. The result of his call was that when the knight returned to his castle, he was a baptized Christian and a follower of "The Way."

Before leaving Rome, however, he bought a slave. He said to the slave, "My brother, you are now free, but I hope it will please you to go home with me and teach my family and all the people in my domain the story of Jesus and The Way."

The face of the former slave lighted up, for he was Brother Marcus, the Christian preacher. He replied, "Gladly will I go with you. I have prayed that I might be allowed to tell the story, and God has answered my prayer."

"We two will make of my kingdom a bit of God's kingdom on earth," said the knight. And so they did. At first the people near the castle listened to Brother Marcus because their master bade them do so, but soon they listened because Brother Marcus told the story of The Way so well. Many of them became Christians, and they came to the castle every week to learn more from Brother Marcus.

When the blessed Christmas season drew near, Brother Marcus told how the season was kept in other countries. The

knight decided that the birthday of the King should be kept in his domain too. A fire blazed on the hearthstone in the great hall. Carolers were everywhere. There was great rejoicing. The feast was ready, and the spirit of love seemed to hover all around.

When the knight and his family came into the room, he noticed a wandering minstrel with a harp, standing in the crowd. The minstrel said, " 'Tis Christmas night, my lord, and I know some ballads of Christmas cheer."

"You shall sing them for us tonight," said the knight.

The feast over, all gathered to hear the minstrel. He sang of the first Christmas night in Bethlehem. Then he sang about a poor woodcutter, who, when he came home one night, heard the cries of a lost child and rescued it. He took the child home to his wife, who cared for it. His children brought gifts to it. They put the child to sleep and then lay down to a well-earned rest. When they awoke the next morning, there was a halo of light where the child had lain, and he stood with his arm outstretched in blessing at the door. It was the Christ child the woodcutter had brought home. Ever after that, good fortune followed the family.

When the minstrel finished this interesting story, everyone asked, "Is the story true?"

"They say it is true; also that every Christmas Eve the Christ child wanders about seeking sweet charity, and that all who take Him in receive His blessing," answered the minstrel.

"How shall we know the Holy Child if He should meet us on the way?" questioned one who had known ill fortune for some time.

"Ah, that is the strange part of it," answered the minstrel. "You have no special way of knowing the Christ child. He will be like any other homeless, forlorn child. It is only after you have ministered to Him that He reveals Himself."

"I cannot fill my house with homeless brats that I find crying by the wayside," said the one who questioned. "But if I knew where to find the Christ child, I would seek Him diligently."

"None can tell us where to find Him, but you can be sure that the Christ child is very near us, especially at Christmas time," answered the minstrel.

"Father," said Rudolph, "it is such a wonderful night. May Felice and I go out and seek a lost child and bring him to our Christmas tree?"

"My son," replied the father, "I do not think that the tale the minstrel sang is true, and I do not believe that the Christ child wanders about over these lonely mountains on Christmas Eve. However, if you wish, you and your sister may go and search."

The two young people started out, but after a long search they turned homeward in disappointment.

In a few minutes they heard a low cry. They plunged into the woods and found a little girl stumbling through the snow, sobbing. As they ran to meet her, she fell, exhausted. Felice gathered the weeping child in her arms and comforted her. "Dear little one, we will take care of you. Do not weep. We will carry you home and put you to sleep in my own warm bed. In the morning you shall go to our Christmas tree, and there will be many gifts for you." They took the child home, wrapped in Rudolph's warm coat.

The smiling servant at the gate gave a cry of surprise when he saw the child, and soon all the household came flocking into the hall, where Felice sat with the child in her arms.

"See, Father! See, Mother! We did find a lost child. May

we keep her to share our Christmas joy? She is so little, so helpless, so dear, and so beautiful," said Felice.

"Of course you may keep her—unless her parents come to claim her," answered her mother.

"Look at the golden hair and blue eyes of this child—so much like the picture of the Christ child that Brother Marcus brought from Rome," suggested one of the maids.

They looked at the painting and found this to be true. A wave of awe swept over the group.

* * * * *

A little serving girl ran to get her most prized possession, a string of gold beads. When she returned, she placed them at the feet of the child, saying, "I will give these for a gift," and her usually dull little face seemed transformed.

All the household began to think of gifts they might make. Finally, one of the maids said to another, "I am sorry I said such hard things to you last week. Please forgive me. That is my gift to this child."

Then one and all spoke kind words and performed gentle deeds as gifts to the child. This they did in memory of the Holy Child, whose birthday they would celebrate on the morrow.

A guest who had sat apart from the rest came forward and said, "I was bent on a horrible deed of vengeance; I will give it up. That is my gift to this child."

All this time, the lord of the castle sat thinking, *I cannot forgive him. He is my great enemy.* But when this man announced that he would not go on with his evil deed, the knight arose, and in a clear voice said, "Then I will not go on with hatred in my heart. In the name of the Holy Child, I forgive my enemy."

Then he sat down and wrote a letter to his enemy, asking him to come and share the Christmas feast in his castle. For the first time in many years, peace seemed to flood his heart.

With the coming of the dawn, carolers sang through the castle the good news, "For unto you is born this day in the city of David a Saviour, which is Christ the Lord."

Brother Marcus, who had been away on

a teaching trip, returned about this time. Seeing the strange, beautiful child, he asked, "Whose child is this?"

Felice told him. "It is a lost child. We found her in the mountains when we went out to find the Christ child."

Brother Marcus replied, "Know this, you are ministering to Christ, for He said, 'Inasmuch as ye have done it unto one of the least of these my brethren, ye have done it unto me.'"

All seemed very happy in the castle, all except the knight who sighed and said to Brother Marcus, "If only my enemy forgives me and comes to the feast, then indeed, you and I will have made a bit of God's kingdom on this mountain."

Soon after, a loud knock was heard at the castle gate. The knight's enemy had accepted the invitation and had come to attend the feast. The knight greeted him, "I bid you welcome."

The stern-faced man replied, "My friend, you are stronger than I. Many times I have wanted to end our useless quarrel, but pride held me back. Even now, I could hardly have accepted your invitation to share in this feast had not a great sorrow filled my heart."

"Perhaps you will find comfort here for your sorrow," said kindly Brother Marcus.

"No, none can give comfort to sorrow like mine," said the man.

"There is One who can comfort all sorrows," replied Brother Marcus.

As they talked, they entered the great hall where the children and others were gathered around the tree. Suddenly, the knight's old enemy gave a loud cry and fell on his knees, "My child! My child!" He stretched his arms out and the child ran to him crying, "Father!"

The man looked at the astonished crowd and said, "My lost child is in my arms again." To the knight he said, "With all my heart I thank you for bidding me to this feast."

The knight replied, "Do not thank me; my children were moved by a tale a wandering minstrel told. They went out to search the mountains for the Christ child."

The man replied, "It is my own child, stolen from me by an enemy, who said I should never see her again. It is the Christ that brought her back to me, and I will worship Him and serve Him forever."

"We gave our gifts to a lost child," whispered the crowd.

Then Brother Marcus's voice sounded above their whispers: "My children, it was to the Christ child that you gave your gifts and your love. Christ is here with you, not only on His blessed birthday but on every day. Do not let His glory depart from this house or from your lives. Let us give thanks and gifts in His name every day."

Mabel Lee Cooper wrote during the first half of the twentieth century.

Celestial Roots

Thomas Vallance

It was in the depths of the Great Depression, Christmas was upon them, and he and his wife owed so much to the storekeeper he couldn't even buy desperately needed groceries.

Suddenly, his horse tripped and fell—

* * * * *

Lighted windows, like low stars, shone from the few scattered buildings of the village. The lone rider didn't look back as he turned his horse and made his way into the darkness.

Ordinarily, to see him ride you would never guess that he was seventy years old. John Verness was a proud old man. But tonight, as he rode in silence across the river bottom, back to his farm, he slumped in the saddle.

The words of the storekeeper, clear in his mind, kept recurring: "You owe me eighty-two dollars now, John. I'm really sorry, but I just can't do it."

The horse's head-down, stumbling walk went unnoticed by the rider. In silent steps it followed the winding path.

Unconsciously, John leaned a gnarled hand on the roll of the saddle for support. What was he going to tell Nora? Things had been going from bad to worse lately, and now Christmas was only ten days away.

He raised troubled eyes to the stars. "I won't tell her," he said with finality. "I just can't." His hand touched the empty grain sack tied to the saddle horn. The piece of paper with the list of most-needed things was still inside.

His fingers tightened on the saddle roll, and his eyes closed for a moment as his thoughts went home. There was perhaps a gallon of kerosene for the lamp, half a bag of flour, some dried garden vegetables, a few potatoes, and little else he could think of.

In a slow, graceful arch, a star was crossing the heavens. John's eyes followed it as he rode. Was there ever such a brilliant star! As though transfixed, John couldn't look away from the heavenly beacon.

That's when, without warning, his horse tripped. With a groan it fell, throwing its rider heavily onto the rough pasture ground. In a flash John knew the horse had tripped on a ground root. Since the last flood wash, they were all over the farm.

The horse struggled to its feet and stood waiting. John rose painfully, thankful no bones were broken. He ran a hand over the horse's legs. Everything seemed all right.

Locating the offending root that crossed the cow path, he tried to pull it loose but could move it only a little. It felt like iron. Thoughtfully he mounted and continued on his way homeward.

In the small kitchen, Nora sat waiting in quiet expectation while John hung his hat and coat on a nail. The lamplight was bright compared to the soft light of the stars.

"Lovely night," said John, walking to the sink and working the cistern pump. He washed, then returned to the table.

Nora glanced at him and rose without responding. "I've

got fresh biscuits ready," she said, walking to the stove. The floor of the old house quivered as she made her way across the room, and the lamp on the table trembled. John looked at it. The shimmering oil in the glass bowl held his eyes. The

image of the storekeeper appeared. John's face was set as he sank wearily into the chair.

"He wouldn't do it!" said Nora, matter-of-factly.

"No," replied John slowly, "he wouldn't do it!"

The yellow lamp light threw his white hair into clear relief as he momentarily bowed his head. After a brief pause, he added, "He says we already owe him too much."

The faint light of a smile touched Nora's eyes as she paused beside him, glancing down. Laying the plate of hot biscuits on the white flower-edged flour-sack tablecloth, she folded her arms thoughtfully. "We'll be all right," she spoke with reassurance. John sat looking at the nearly empty sugar bowl.

Nora tilted her head. "Jim Slater said he would take the calf as soon as it is weaned, and veal is a good price."

Slowly she turned toward the stove to hide the tears in her eyes. The little calf was her pet, the last of a fine herd.

John sat staring dejectedly into one of the dark corners of the kitchen as Nora cleared the meager table and brought the worn Bible from its place and laid it in front of him for their accustomed devotions. Mechanically, John took the treasured book, and it fell open to a passage in Matthew. After a moment he began to read in a quiet voice, "Now when Jesus was

born in Bethlehem of Judea in the days of Herod the king, behold, there came wise men from the east to Jerusalem."

The beautiful Christmas story unfolded in that dimly lit room as the white-haired man read on. "And lo, the star which they saw in the east, went before them." Suddenly, John stopped his reading and closed the pages.

"Why, what is it, John?" Nora inquired, puzzled by the strange look on her husband's face.

"I just thought of something. I have to go out for a while. I'll be back soon. Don't worry." And he grabbed his coat and hat and closed the door hastily behind him.

John first went to the woodshed and picked up the axe and saw. Then he turned toward the dark pasture through which he had recently ridden. He knew he could easily wait till morning, but for some unexplainable reason this just had to be done now.

The sharp axe bounced off the tough root, but he was persistent. On one knee he worked in silence.

When he finally had freed the twisted root from the earth, he sat looking at it. It was very heavy, and smooth as glass. Holding it up, he turned it first one way and then another. Each turn brought a new image to his mind.

John stood up and began walking slowly back to the house. From time to time he stopped and held the root up to look at it again. It seemed to glisten as though reflecting a ray of light. John glanced at the sky. Nothing there but that one bright star.

Nora said little during the next few days as John cut and carved. She smiled often as she worked and offered occasional helpful suggestions as her husband carved with tense care. Finally, he was finished, but rest would not come. He carved

another figure, and another.

Then one day he saddled up and rode in to see Cal, the storekeeper, carrying one of the carvings carefully before him across the saddle.

"How are you, John?" greeted Cal. The storekeeper's eyes focused on the carving. John held it out. Cal took it, turning it appraisingly.

"Did *you* do this, John?" he asked in wonderment.

"Yes," replied John, simply, but pleased. "Thought you might have a sale for such, Cal. People are always looking for something new," he added, hopefully.

"Ain't any hard wood ever grew around here, John," mused Cal in deep thought. "The grain is so even, not twisted like other roots. It's more like ebony." They stood in silence in the presence of the unknown.

"Set any price on it, John?" smiled Cal.

"Whatever the trade will stand, Cal. I'll leave it with you," he said and hurried out.

* * * * *

When Christmas Eve came, John could stand the suspense no longer. Harnessing up, he and Nora drove into town. As he entered the little settlement, a tenseness came over him. In front of the store, he glanced at Nora.

"You go, John," she smiled. She didn't want to see him hurt.

As he opened the door with a feeling of timidity, he resolutely braced up. After all, it was Christmas Eve! Then, for a moment, he stood drinking in the pleasing odors of a country store—apples, ginger biscuits, cheese—all so good.

"Merry Christmas, John," Cal called with a friendly wave. There was a broad smile on the storekeeper's face. "Sold that carving," he beamed. "A lady from the city passed through yesterday. She said it was a rare piece of creative genius—said it was beautiful!" Cal reached into a drawer and laid a brand-new twenty-dollar bill on the counter. "There's the money she gave me. Said she could use more if you've got them. Merry Christmas, John!"

John, in spite of all the hopes he had cherished, was stunned with his sudden good fortune. Finally he stammered,

"Thanks, Cal. Thanks!"

Hurrying through the doorway, John looked up at the clear sky. His eyes again fell upon the star—the bright one he had seen on that dark night when his horse had stumbled over the protruding root. It could be the Christmas Star!

"Merry Christmas!" he murmured excitedly and then hurried to the buggy to tell Nora.

———————

Thomas Vallance wrote for magazines during the second half of the twentieth century.

A Story for Christmas

Jody Shields

They had so little money and they received so few gifts, yet she wanted to give her beloved mother something both memorable and valuable. Was that impossible, as poor as they were?

* * * * *

We were not, as my brother Fred used to say, "exactly the poorest family in the community"; then he would add, "but it's for certain we aren't the richest, either." We had most of the necessities, but the extras were few and spaced far between. So it was that by comparison, our Christmases were rather lean.

I remember we used to stare wide-eyed with awe and wonder at the stacks of packages under the Christmas trees at our cousins' homes. All around the bases of their trees would be richly and fashionably wrapped presents—and it wouldn't even be Christmas for another week.

At our house, Santa brought everything on Christmas Eve. There just weren't any other presents to be had, except what we gave each other. They were usually things we made ourselves, and we kept them secreted away until Christmas Eve. Then we would get them out and place them in a chair near the tree so Santa could distribute them with the bounty he brought when he came.

On Christmas Day we would open our presents, wild with excitement and delight. As soon as everything had been opened, inspected, and given an initial breaking-in, we were off for our cousins' houses to see how they had fared. Somehow, looking at all their treasures made ours seem pale by comparison. We always took fruitcakes, homemade candy and cookies to them. Almost always they gave us grocery boxes of oranges, nuts, and canned goods.

The Christmas I remember best was just before I turned eight. My older sister, Marcia, was ten, and she had learned to crochet during the summer. She announced with a great deal of pride that she was going to crochet Mom a pair of hot pads made like little girls' dresses. She had been saving her allowance for the yarn, and she had asked her Primary teacher to help her with the pattern.

I was really impressed and wished I knew how to do something really beautiful like that. All I could do was some embroidery, but I didn't really enjoy doing it. Besides, I didn't have the kind of money it would take to make a scarf or a pair of pillow slips.

Christmas was drawing closer, and we were busy getting things ready. Almost every night we would shut ourselves in our bedroom and work on the gifts we were making for everyone. Marcia would be crocheting as swiftly as she could, being very careful to keep her stitches even and not to miss any. I would sit on our bed and watch her and wish I had something special for Mom, but I could think of nothing.

One day, I had gone through some boxes on the back

73

porch to see if I could find some odds and ends to trim the book tote I was making for Marcia. Mom had said she would help me sew them on if I could find some scraps and cut out the designs.

In one of the boxes I found an old picture frame. The glass had been broken out, but there were still the backing pieces of cardboard and a torn, yellowing piece of paper in it. I recognized it immediately, and it gave me a sharp twinge of regret when I remembered how it had come to be hidden away in the scrap box.

On the paper was a poem surrounded with drawings of flowers, birds, a small house, clouds, and grass. It had hung in the kitchen ever since I could remember, and we children had read and reread the poem so many times we all had it memorized. Then, one day, we were fighting and chasing each other with the broom, and I accidentally knocked the picture to the floor. The glass broke into a hundred pieces, and some of them had torn the paper on which the poem was written.

Mom had come quickly. At first she didn't say anything. She just stood there for a minute with a strange look on her face. Then she quietly shooed us out of the room so we wouldn't get cut on the broken glass. It was so unusual for her not to say something that we went in a hurry but lingered at the doorway.

We looked back to see her on her knees picking up the broken pieces of glass, and we could tell that she was crying.

She never said anything about it. Not even when Daddy got home from work that night. He didn't seem to notice that the picture was gone. All during dinner we couldn't keep from stealing guilty glances at the spot where it had hung, all the time expecting Mother to mention it and Father to take proper disciplinary measures. But nothing was said; the frame and torn paper had just disappeared as if they had never existed.

Now, as I held them in my hands with a wave of memories sweeping over me, I knew what I was going to do for my gift to Mom this year. Very carefully I wrapped the frame in the scraps I had picked out for the book tote and carried it to my room. I hid it in the bottom of my drawer, underneath my pajamas, until I could assemble the materials I would need.

I would have to have Daddy or Wayne, my oldest brother, cut a new sheet of glass for me. In order to get the right size, I would have to measure the cardboard backing. I made a mental note to do that first. Then I would have to find a piece of paper to do the printing and drawings on. It had to be special paper,

heavier than most, with a silky finish. It never occurred to me to doubt whether I could copy the printing and the drawing accurately enough to be acceptable. I just knew that this was what I had to do for my mother for Christmas.

The next time we went to town for groceries, I left the family and hurried to the dime store where Mom did much of her shopping. I knew they had a stationery department, and I was sure that was where I would find the paper I needed. The clerk was very helpful, and together we found just the right piece of paper. But it came in a package, and if I bought the whole package, I wouldn't have enough money for the gold ink I would need. I had to have gold ink because that is what was on the other one. It was such a good idea that to do it only halfway would be worse than not to do it at all. I would just have to get more money. But, how, this close to Christmas?

A fat, wet tear slipped from my eye and ran down my cheek.

"What's wrong?" asked the kindly clerk. "Isn't this paper what you wanted?"

"Yes, yes," I replied, trying vainly to hold back the other tears that were pushing to spill out after the first, "only—only I don't have enough money to buy the whole package and gold ink too," I sobbed.

"Hmm." The clerk tapped her chin with a forefinger. "Would it help if you bought only one sheet?" She smiled. "I could sell you one sheet for a nickel."

"Oh, yes!" I breathed happily, wiping my tears on the sleeve of my coat. I handed her my money, and she took one sheet of paper from the package and put the rest of the package in a special place under the counter. She got a small jar of gold ink and rang up the sale on her cash register.

Clutching the sack she had handed me, I hurried back to the grocery store just as the family was about to launch an all-out search for me.

"Where have you been?" they asked. "We were terribly worried about you."

"I was just doing some shopping," I said.

Since everyone was feeling the spirit of Christmas, no one said any more about it, and we went home.

I went straight to the bedroom where I had been assembling all the things I would need. I had only two days left until Christmas. I would have to hurry. I would also have to be very careful in my haste to keep from spoiling it. To make mistakes would be worse than not to do it at all, I told myself as I got out pencil, pen, and scrap paper. School was out for the Christmas holiday, so I was able to spend most of the day working on my gift. Marcia had finished her hot pads and had them wrapped and hidden away until Christmas. She was free to play in the snow, or ice skate, or whatever her fancy dictated. And her fancy certainly didn't relish watching me prepare my gift. She didn't know what it was going to be, and I didn't want her to know. I didn't want *anyone* to know. I thought they might laugh and say it was silly.

Very carefully I practiced each drawing over and over until I felt I could do it well enough to set it down on the silk-surfaced sheet. I drew the pictures lightly in pencil and then outlined them in India ink. The gold would provide accents and be the finishing touch.

The next day I began the lettering. First I practiced copying each line over and over until my fingers hurt. Then I rested for a while before I started lightly penciling the letters on the sheet with the drawings.

I had had some doubt about my ability to print the letters small enough and neatly enough, but as I stared at the torn original, I realized that it, too, had been printed by hand, and I felt that if they (whoever "they" may have been) could do it, so could I.

I dipped the pen in the ink and sent up a silent prayer, *Dear, dear God, please let it be neat. Please don't let me spoil it now.* I drew the first letter with its fancy curlicues and thicker lines, and sighed audibly as it came out perfect. The other letters were plainer, but smaller, and they must be kept of uniform size. I paused to rest, dipped the pen, uttered my prayer silently in my mind, and set down the other two letters in the first word, then the rest of the letters in the first line, and so on. Very carefully and cautiously I drew over each letter with black ink, praying that it wouldn't smear; praying that it wouldn't drip; praying that the lines wouldn't waver; praying that it would be a worthy gift.

At last it was finished. I put on the touches of gold and left it to dry for a minute while I got out the frame and the new glass and the wrapping paper. Then, I slipped the glass into the frame, set the sheet with the poem against the glass, put the cardboard backing in place, and tapped the small nails into the holes to hold it all together.

I wrapped tissue paper around it, then placed it in an emptied Christmas card box and wrapped it. It was Christmas Eve, and my fingers hurt, my shoulders ached, and my eyes burned from the strain, but my gift for Mom was ready, and my heart was light as I left the bedroom and closed the door softly behind me.

* * * * *

The next morning I could hardly open my presents, I was so excited and somewhat apprehensive. I kept close watch on Mom as she opened her gifts. She smiled a big smile and gave Marcia a special hug when she unwrapped the hot pads. *They were really something,* I thought, with a twinge of uncertainty.

At last she was opening the package that held my gift. My breath caught in my throat. It seemed everyone was watching, and I couldn't help wishing they wouldn't pay any attention. Mom carefully drew aside the tissue paper and looked at the framed poem, the crude drawings, the rough printing. For a long moment she sat staring at it,

then she slowly threw back her head and I sensed, more than heard, a sob catch in her throat.

I was intently avoiding looking at her. I directed my full attention to the new pair of ice skates I had received for Christmas, yet I knew that Mom threw me a look out of the corner of her eye as she rose and carried the gift, box and all, into the kitchen.

"She's crying," Marcia said softly. "Why?"

"I don't know," Fred answered easily, not bothering to take his eyes off the electric train set he was trying to assemble around the base of the Christmas tree.

I assiduously avoided answering and looked the other way as I wiped a tear from my own cheek. Suddenly, I couldn't stay there any longer. I grabbed my new skates and my coat and ran outside. Everyone would think I had gone to try the skates. I ran through the snow with tears blinding my eyes. My precious, rotten, horrible gift had been rejected, and it served me right! I collapsed sobbing on the tree trunk where we sat to change our skates, the image of Mother throwing my gift into the trash, box and all, vivid in my mind.

Daddy found me there. He had followed Mom into the kitchen and then had followed me outside. "What's wrong, Kitten?" he asked gently, as he pressed my head against his shoulder so the rough weave of his jacket could absorb my tears.

"She didn't like it!" I sobbed in my misery.

"Nonsense!" he replied quickly. "Honey, she *loved* it. Believe me, Kitten. I don't think she has ever received a gift that pleased her more."

"Then why is she crying?"

"I doubt you'd understand." He paused so long I was afraid he wasn't going to try to explain. After a long minute, which I spent drying my eyes and blowing my nose, he went on. "You see, Kitten, that poem was given as a gift to your grandmother many years ago. When our first baby was born, Grandma gave it to your mom. She said that Mamma should always remember the message of the poem, and that if she did, it would help and inspire her as much as it had helped and inspired Grandma. Mamma had me hang it in the kitchen where she would be able to see it and read its message. She loved it very much."

"Then why didn't she get it fixed when we broke it?" I asked, not yet convinced.

"Well, it bothered Mamma to love that particular picture so much. She hated to make a big fuss over it. You see, Kitten, *she* was the one who gave it to Grandma in the first place!"

He took my hand, and together we walked slowly to the house. Inside it was cozy and warm, and the fragrance of the Christmas turkey was beginning to spread from the oven. There was Mamma, her eyes shining as she stood against the sink peeling potatoes. Marcia was gathering the wrapping paper and ribbon from the living-room floor. Fred and Wayne were arguing (quietly yet) over the electric train, and there was my gift, hanging on the wall in the exact spot where it had hung for so long—ever since I could remember.

Jody Shields wrote for magazines during the second half of the twentieth century.

The Baby Camel That Walked to Jesus

Walter A. Dyer

For two thousand years, this Nativity story has been told and retold by Syrian parents to their children.
Now the story has come west.
It is a story children will love.

* * * * *

This is the story that old Abd-el-Atti told to little Hamzi as they sat cross-legged before a small fire of charcoal on the roof of their house in the Syrian village of Hâsbeiyâ, looking across the pleasant olive groves and terraced vineyards and the fruitful little river Hâsbânî beneath the snowy turban of Mount Hermon and on to the sharp, barren ridge of Jebel-ez-Zohr.

Like all people in those days, the Magi watched for the coming of the Messiah. And because they were astrologers, it was the heavens they searched, looking for a sign.

One night—the night the Christ child was born—the wise men among the Magi discovered a light in the sky, which some took to be a comet and some a very bright star. These Magi were very learned and knew all the stars, so the appearance of the new light puzzled them, until God revealed to one of them in a vision that what they saw was not a star at all, but an angel with a torch, ready to lead them to the spot where the infant Messiah lay.

The holy man who had first seen the light looked at it again, and lo! it had moved westward. He told his brethren about the movement of the light, and the three most wise and devout among them resolved to follow the light whithersoever it might lead them.

Now, Melik, the holy man to whom the birth of the Child had been revealed, had a favorite camel. She was not a gentle camel. She bit viciously with her strong front teeth any camels and horses and people who came near—and even Melik sometimes. She could have kicked with her forefeet also, but she could do more damage with her teeth. She was a mean, ill-natured, exceedingly stupid animal, as indeed most camels are. But she was of the ancient lineage of the Maharai and was strong and of great endurance. She could store away more food and drink in her hump than any other camel Melik had ever known. No sandstorm could weaken her, no day was too hot, no journey too long. Always swift and powerful, she would swing along bearing her burden, so Melik chose her to carry him.

Melik threw richly woven rugs over her back. On her head he placed a tasseled headdress, and about her neck a new prayer rope made of many-colored strands and tied with the sacred knot so that its tassel hung nearly to her knees. Her own coat was a rich, dark brown, and she looked very handsome in all this finery.

* * * * *

Just as Melik was finishing the preparations for their journey, he felt a light touch on his thigh. Looking down, he saw a little camel calf about three feet high. It was a light cream color and had soft eyes the color of strained honey. Then he remembered: a son had been born to his camel on the morning he had first discovered the new light in the heavens. His mind had been so occupied with other things that he had forgotten about it.

The baby camel had been standing on his weak little legs in a corner of the courtyard, perplexed and alarmed by the bustle of preparation. Even his own mother looked strange and a bit frightful to him in her bright trappings. But at length loneliness and hunger overcame his fear, and he came timidly up, his eyes big with wonder, and slipped in close to his mother's side.

Now Melik was a humane man. He knew that a baby camel couldn't leave its mother until it was a year old, and he knew that one as young as this one would certainly perish if left alone. Yet he felt that he must ride the mother as the quest was important and she was the only camel he had that he felt sure would carry him as far as he needed to go. So, eventually, and with great misgivings, he decided to let the baby camel go along too, since it seemed that the only thing he knew how to do was to trot along close to his mother. Then Melik made a little prayer rope for the calf and knotted it about his neck.

The news of the heavenly light had spread all over the countryside, and there were hundreds and thousands of people who wanted to accompany the three holy priests of the Magi on their journey. When they started, other holy men and hundreds of soldiers joined them, until there was a great army. Some rode horses and some marched on foot, but the three Magi who led them all rode on camels, and the little cream-colored calf trotted along beside them.

At length they came to the great river that is called Euphrates, and men were sent up and down the river banks looking for a ford where they might cross, for it was the season of rains, and the river was swollen and turbulent.

While they were waiting, God showed the three wise men what a foolish thing it was for so many to follow the quest. The people in the countries through which they passed might think they were an army of invasion and rise up in arms against them. Besides, the journey bade fair to be a long one, and it was becoming increasingly difficult to find food for so many men and horses and camels. So the three Magi picked a retinue of one thousand, and left all the others—seven times one thousand—on the east bank of the Euphrates, to return to their homes.

* * * * *

Then the three Magi and the retinue of one thousand began to ford the river, the horses swimming and the camels wading in the shallowest place. But the snows were melting on Hermon, and the great river was rushing so fast that it was foaming, and the noise made by the water terrified the little camel, which could neither swim nor wade. So he ran up and down the river's bank, bleating because he feared that his mother and Melik and all the host were about to desert him. He was too small and weak to trust himself to the ford;

he thought he would surely drown.

The little camel's mother refused to leave her calf behind. When Melik saw what the trouble was, he dismounted and then he and one of the other men tied the baby camel securely to its mother's back, and that's how he crossed safely, though much frightened.

* * * * *

For many days and nights the party traveled, and the little camel, trotting beside his mother, grew very weary. He didn't understand the reason for this pressing on day after day. There were places where he would have preferred to kneel down and rest, but his mother kept swinging steadily on, and he had no choice but to follow. His head reached scarcely above his mother's knees, and much of the time all he could see was a forest of long, striding legs, with sometimes a glimpse of the flowing tails of the horses and the white robes of the Magi.

There was much rain and cold wind, and men and horses suffered. At night, the Magi pitched their

tents on the wet ground and fed the camels straw and beans that had been moistened and pounded and kneaded together, for there was very little of the food of green leaves and shoots and twigs of thorny shrubs that camels love to eat. The camels slept, resting on the great pads on their knees and chest, and the baby camel knelt close to his mother, out of the wind, to keep as warm and dry as he could.

The caravan passed through the pleasant valley, across the barren plain, up into the rocky, desolate passes of the mountains and then down on the other side. At one place they could find no wood for their fires, so they sent out scouts, who brought back great bundles of wild grapevine, and these they burned to cook their suppers and dry their cloaks. That is why to this day a fire of vine stems is kindled on the night of the Nativity in the middle of the Syrian church at Ourfa.

Past the purple mountains of Moab and Gilead they journeyed, and then down, down into the great, desolate valley of the salty Dead Sea and the jungle of the River Jordan. The Jordan is not like the rivers of Damascus—it is rapid and treacherous and difficult to cross. The jungle, too, is full of reptiles and wild beasts. In the night, the baby camel would sometimes hear in the distance a terrible deep roar that set him trembling and crouching closer to his mother.

But the Magi followed the light in the sky, surviving the dangers of the valley and arriving at the city of Jericho, where now only a village stands in the midst of a more fruitful country. Here they rested a day and a night, and the camels chewed their cuds in peace. The baby camel had sore need of this rest, for his little legs were weak, and though he carried no burden, he was nearly spent. Day after day he had stayed at his mother's side, wondering if he must always keep up this

weary trotting, knowing not whither he was going nor why. If he had not been born with the blood and bone of the Maharai, he would have collapsed. But the day after their rest, they made him get up again and follow them through a dreary land where the soldiers of the retinue had need to be on the watch for robbers.

The star was leading the Magi southward now, and at length they came to the great city of Jerusalem. They sent couriers before them to inform Herod, the king, that theirs was a friendly pilgrimage, and he received the wise men of the East and did them honor.

When the children of Herod saw the baby camel, they were filled with delight. They decked him gorgeously in scarlet and purple and white, and they put a gold chain around his neck. He could not eat their sweetmeats, but they taught him to drink water colored with grape juice and sweetened with honey. The baby camel thought he must have come at last to the end of his long journey, and he was very happy.

On the way from Jericho the clouds had obscured the light that led the Magi, so they made inquiries in Jerusalem. Herod told them the news of the birth of a child in Bethlehem of Judea, the city of Ruth and of David, and he bade them go and then return to him with news of what they found.

* * * * *

It was only a little way to Bethlehem—six or seven miles to the south of Jerusalem—and the three wise priests, wishing to finish their quest alone, left their retinue in the city and started out at sunrise. The baby camel was sleeping peacefully on a little bed of straw, but when he heard his mother call, he

felt that he must obey, though he knew not why. He arose to his feet with a sigh and walked into the courtyard, where Melik took off the golden chain and the fine linen that the children of the king had put upon him. Then they took up their march again, three camels stolid from experience, three wise men wrapped in thought, and a baby camel, trotting wearily by his mother's side and gazing with inquiring eyes upon a strange world.

Bethlehem, the "House of Bread," lies on a double hill with a pleasant valley between it and Jerusalem. The road the Magi took lay along a curving ridge. When they had gone part way, they came to the hill Mâr Elyâs, and here they stopped at a spring to get water. The little camel drank thirstily with the rest, and the place is called the "Well of the Magi" to this day.

From this hill they could see both Jerusalem and the little town of Bethlehem, each hidden from the other. To the east they looked afar off across the valleys to where they caught glimpses of the blue Dead Sea, and within their view were olive orchards and stony sheep pastures on the hillsides.

The sky had cleared, and it was here that the wise men observed the angel's torch shining brighter than ever in the broad day. Only it did not travel before them now, but stood still over Bethlehem.

They started on again, and as they drew near to the town they passed among the rocky ridges and ravines where David had kept his sheep before he went forth to slay Goliath, and where the shepherds had been watching their flocks on the night of the Nativity. They moved forward with more rapidity now, the camels seeming to realize as well as the men that they were nearing their journey's end.

The baby camel seemed drawn irresistibly toward Bethlehem.

Perhaps there were children there who also had soft hands and sweetened water. He trotted along quite blithely as his mother quickened her pace.

* * * * *

When the three wise men of the East at last reached Bethlehem, they inquired the way to the house of Josef ben David, as King Herod had directed them to do. There they found the Child with His mother. Taking rich offerings of gold and sweet-smelling frankincense and myrrh, they went in to do Him homage, leaving the camels kneeling outside.

Now an old camel will stay where it is put, especially when it is tired, because it is too stupid to do anything else. But the baby camel was filled with curiosity and wanted to follow the Magi into the house. However, to his great disappointment, the gate was closed. Then, being very weary, he lay down beside his mother and moaned and bleated piteously.

Inside the house, where the Magi were kneeling and offering their gifts, the Child heard the moaning of the little camel that was denied the sight of Him after coming so far, and He lifted His tiny hand. At this the gate opened, and the baby camel walked in on his tired, wobbly legs and stood looking at the Christ child with great wonder in his soft eyes.

The Child smiled and raised His hand again and thus blessed the little camel, who went out to be happy and to live forever and never to be cross and vicious like other camels.

So now, when Christmastime comes around, the American children at the mission receive gifts from Santa Claus. And Gaghant Bab puts sweetmeats in a box for the Armenian boys and girls. But Syrian children who have been good for a

year and a day and who leave a dish of sweetened water outside the door on the night of the Nativity may find on Christmas morning candies and pretty toys and jars of pomegranate jelly that have been left by the little camel that walked to Jesus.

Walter A. Dyer (1878–1943) was a prolific author of books and stories. He specialized in books about dogs—books such as *Gulliver the Great and Other Dog Stories* and *Pierrot, Dog of Belgium*. He was also long-time director of Amherst College Press.

Choices

Isobel Stewart

Christmas on her own—it was something Rachel had neither anticipated nor planned for. So what should she do with it?

* * * * *

Christmas wasn't an easy time for Rachel. But now, four years after her divorce, she could look back and tell herself that with each year, it became a little less difficult.

The first Christmas without Brad she could hardly bear her unhappiness. But the sight of Rebecca quickly brushing aside a tear, and of Tim, only six then, unable to hide his bewilderment when he opened his father's present to him, somehow helped Rachel find the strength to hide her own sorrow.

The next year, things had been a little easier. By then, she had learned to accept that, although their marriage was over, Brad's love and concern for their children was as strong as ever. She learned to accept, too, her children's weekend visits to their father—and his new wife.

In those awful early days of coming to terms with the end of her marriage, Rachel had to keep reminding herself that Brad had known Jenny long before he had met her. Known her, and lost her, and found her again, when he was already married to Rachel. Rebecca had been seven, and Tim five.

For months Brad had tried to maintain their marriage and to forget Jenny, but he hadn't succeeded.

All this she had learned to live with; but now, when Brad's job had taken him to the other side of the world and visits were so few, how could she agree to his request to let Rebecca and Tim spend Christmas with him, Jenny—and their new baby, Michael.

Dismayed, Rachel could only listen to this man who had been her husband, who was her children's father, who surely must know just how much he was asking of her.

"It would mean everything to Jenny and me, Rachel," he said. "Won't you ask Rebecca and Tim? See how they feel?"

"Christmas?" She sighed. She knew she was playing for time. "I don't know, Brad. Their friends are here. We do things together in the Christmas holidays. Rebecca is twelve now, you know."

The silence stretched over the miles between them.

"I know that, Rachel," he said, so sadly that in spite of everything, her heart went out to him. "Won't you at least tell them that I would like them to come to us for Christmas?"

And when she did, there was no doubt about what her answer would have to be—Rebecca's eyes shone, Tim's face lit up. But she saw the wordless, swift agreement that passed between them.

"No, Mum, we wouldn't want you to be alone at Christmas," Rebecca said, speaking for both of them. "We could go to visit Dad and Jenny some other time—in the summer, maybe." She held her small chin high. "Anyway, we'd rather be at home with you for Christmas, wouldn't we, Tim."

"Oh, yes, Mum, we'd rather be with you," he agreed.

Her children shouldn't have to make these choices, Rachel thought miserably to herself. "I'll be fine," she told them. "It's only for ten days. You'll be home before I know it."

That night she let Rebecca and Tim phone their father to tell him. Resolutely, she kept herself busy in the kitchen, waiting for the call to end.

"Dad's very pleased," Tim told her. "And do you know what? Michael is almost walking. Dad thinks maybe he'll walk while we're there."

Rebecca quelled him with a glance.

As Rachel handed them each their plates of pasta, she was pleased to notice that her hands were steady.

"That's good," she replied equably. "You were both over a year old before you walked.

"It's only a month away," she went on briskly. "We'll have to start thinking about what clothes you'll take with you."

Over breakfast one morning early in December, Tim asked her if she would go to the midnight carol service.

Rachel's heart lurched. Go alone? No, she couldn't. But two pairs of eyes were watching her anxiously.

"Yes, I probably will," she fibbed casually.

"You could go with the Johnsons," Rebecca suggested.

"Yes, of course I could," Rachel agreed carefully. But she knew she couldn't do that. How could she go with a family, with children the same ages as Tim and Rebecca, knowing that after the midnight service they would go home together, and in the morning sit in front of the fire, Jim and Meg in their dressing gowns, while the children opened their stockings . . .

85

***** *

Determined not to cast any shadow over her children's excitement, Rachel helped them to decide on presents to take for their father, Jenny, and the baby, assuring Rebecca that little Michael would love the blue teddy, and agreeing with Tim that his father would think the book about vintage cars perfect.

"At least you'll have Rusty for company," Rebecca said one day. The yellow Labrador wagged his tail at the mention of his name.

Under her lashes, Rebecca looked searchingly at her mother and said, "And if he isn't well, you can just take him to Steve."

Rachel felt her cheeks color. "You know Rusty is hardly ever unwell," she pointed out.

"Yes, but Steve likes it when you have to take him to be checked over," her daughter answered demurely.

Steve was Rusty's vet. He was a few years older than Rachel, and a widower, with no children. He ran his practice from his home, just round the corner from them, and she and the children had become friendly with him over the last four years.

Rachel knew very well, although nothing had ever been said, that Steve would like their friendship to move on. Sometimes she thought she would like that too. He was easy to be with, and when he joined her and the children for a walk along the shore—Rusty running ahead of them—she found herself very close to responding to the question in his eyes.

On one such occasion Rebecca had told him that she and Tim were looking for a double-sunrise shell, because Mum had always wanted one.

"So what does this special shell look like, Rachel?" he had asked her.

"It's like a butterfly," she said. "Both sides are marked with the same pattern of white and three rosy rays fanning out from the golden hinge that holds the two sides together. Years ago I read about it in a book called *Gift From the Sea*. It's unusual here, and very fragile." She smiled. "I don't suppose I'll ever find one."

"Oh, I think you will," Steve said. "Don't give up, Rachel." She had had the strong certainty that he wasn't just speaking about her shell.

She thought about that as the time for her children to leave drew closer. She had moved on. She had managed to let go of Brad. But in doing so, she had found a comfort zone she could live within. To move beyond that would take more courage than she had.

Having to face Christmas alone, without Rebecca and Tim, was a challenge—one she didn't think she would be able to rise to.

***** *

A week before the children were due to leave, Rebecca asked Rachel what she would do on Christmas Day.

"I haven't decided yet," she said. "Auntie Jill has asked me to spend the day with them, but I'm not too keen on the drive. I could go on Christmas Eve, of course, and stay over. Maybe I'll do that."

The next day, she had just come home from work when the doorbell rang. She opened the door to find Steve there.

Rusty greeted him with great enthusiasm. Steve patted

him. "I hear you'll be on your own for Christmas," he said. "Rebecca came in to look at the Siamese kittens I was telling her about. She told me." He looked straight at her, his grey eyes direct. "She's worried about you, Rachel."

"I know," Rachel replied. "I'll be fine, Steve."

"My brother lives on a farm an hour away," he continued. "I'll be spending Christmas Day with them—his wife and their three kids. It's always noisy, but it's fun. Jeff and Helen would love to have you join us, Rachel."

"I don't think so, Steve," she said quickly. "But thank you for asking me."

Steve glanced at his watch, spoke about a house call he had to make, and stood up.

"I thought you might say that," he said. "If you change your mind, just let me know."

* * * * *

A few days before Christmas, Rachel drove the children to the airport. Tim was unable to hide his excitement, and Rebecca tried hard to conceal hers.

"You're going to have a wonderful time," Rachel said brightly. She hugged them both, and Rebecca reassured her that they would phone as soon as they arrived.

"Will Dad be at the airport to meet us?" Tim asked for the umpteenth time.

Rachel's heart lurched at the thought of Brad seeing them for the first time in months.

"Of course. Off you go," she told them. "And have a lovely Christmas."

She managed to make it back to the car before the tears came. Rusty, who had been sitting in the backseat, took a chance and moved forward, trying to comfort her, his big golden head pushing anxiously against her.

"You silly old dog," Rachel said to him. She found herself smiling as she dried her tears. The thought of going back to the empty house was suddenly more than she could take, so instead she drove straight to the beach.

It was cold and blustery as the waves pounded the shore, and the long stretch of sand was deserted.

Rachel buttoned up her jacket, pulled on the extra gloves she kept in the car, and set off with Rusty bounding ahead of her. His tail wagged hopefully as he waited for her to throw a stick for him.

On the third throw, Rachel stopped and looked down at the wet sand. It couldn't be, it couldn't possibly be . . . But it was. Her double-sunrise shell, unbroken by the rough seas that had thrown it onto the shore.

She picked it up and looked at it. It was perfect—just as she had described it to Steve.

The two halves matched perfectly, rosy rays fanning out. In spite of the cold wind, she took off her gloves and held the shell in her hand.

I have it, she thought, *my perfect double-sunrise shell. Who would have believed it?*

With that, her thoughts turned to the empty house, the lonely Christmas ahead of her. And slowly, on that cold, deserted beach, with the wind blowing around her, and grey waves breaking on the shore, she saw the choices that lay before her. She could spend the rest of her life feeling sorry for herself, . . . afraid to reach out. Or she could create her own sunrise.

Carefully, she tucked her precious shell into her pocket, put her gloves back on, and with Rusty running ahead, she turned and walked back to her car.

She was going to ring the Johnsons and ask if she could go with them to the midnight service. And then she was going to ring Steve and tell him that she had changed her mind; she would love to spend Christmas Day with him. She would tell him that she had found her shell.

And later that night, when the children phoned, they would be pleased to hear that she certainly wasn't going to spend Christmas all alone.

Isobel Stewart, of Helderberg, South Africa, passed away in 2012. She was one of the world's most renowned short-story writers, publishing more than fifteen hundred stories, and having fifty full-length books to her credit.

The Dream Catcher

Joseph Leininger Wheeler

She thunders by with splendid speed—
An avalanche of fire and steel,
Whose tempest strokes of whirring wheel
Beat like the hoofs of Neptune's steed;
Cleaving the dark in mighty flight,
A raging monster, driving fast,
A harnessed earthquake reeling past,
Through the long reach of murky might!

—*"The Midnight Limited," by C. F. Finley*

When the Midnight Limited comes through in the middle of the night, it shakes the house. At first, she awakens in terror and cries out, "Daddy! Daddy!" But in time, she gets used to it. Eventually, it never awakens her at all—the midnight visitor but the fabric of night. And with Daddy there, what could possibly hurt her?

* * * * *

Thanksgiving is over, and Questa's fifth Christmas is just around the corner. And how Daddy loves Christmas!

The day after "Gratitude Day," as he called it, his Christmas tree would be the first on the block to be hauled into the house, set up, and decorated—with Mommy's help, while Questa continually gets in the way. But nobody is cross with her. Instead, Daddy whirls her—his ecstatic daughter—around like she's the sails to his ship, and all the time he's singing the happiest Christmas songs he knows. Mommy always has stars in her love-lit eyes when Daddy is home, even though they've been married for more than six and a half years now. Apparently, nobody has ever told her that honeymoons last only a year.

Then, just a few days later, Daddy comes home in the middle of the day—something he's never done before. Mother's eyes, as always, glow when he enters the house, but the glow quickly fades as she is struck by the stark pain she sees there. "Robert!" she cries. "What's wrong?"

Robert does nothing to prepare them for the next six words. He just speaks them out in all their ugly threat: "The Japanese have bombed Pearl Harbor!"

Mother's hands fly to her cheeks, she cries out in horror, "Oh no! Oh no! . . . What will happen now?"

Instead of answering, Robert strides over to their new radio and turns it on. He gets only static at first, but then they hear the story that will be repeated endlessly throughout the day and the days that follow:

At 7:58 this morning, the Pacific Fleet of the United States was literally and figuratively caught sleeping. Reason being: the United States wasn't at war with anyone. Suddenly, and without any warning at all, the dawn skies over Hawaii's Pearl Harbor were filled with

attacking planes—high-level bombers, dive bombers, and fighter planes launched from Japanese aircraft carriers three hundred miles away. Amazingly, no one had noticed the invading fleet.

Most of the officers and men on the battleship U.S.S. Arizona were aboard when the attacking planes began ripping it apart. Of its crew of fourteen hundred, 1,103 were killed. The dreadnought U.S.S. Oklahoma was next: a few minutes after eight A.M., three huge torpedoes smashed into its hull, and in no time at all, the ship rolled over, completely destroyed. The attacks were unrelenting; no sooner had one wave of planes done its worst when another wave took its place; then another; and another. For two nightmarish hours the attacks continued.

Then, just as suddenly as it began, it is over. America's great Pacific Fleet now lies in ruins. More than two thousand Navy men are dead and seven hundred are wounded. The Army and Marines report an additional 327 killed and 433 wounded—besides civilians.

As post-attack shock waves reverberate across the nation, little else is done. Radios are left on as further bulletins come in. Three days later, in pain-wracked somber sentences, President Franklin Roosevelt, speaking before both houses of Congress, says that Sunday, December 7, 1941, is "a date that will live in infamy!" Six and a half minutes later, Congress declares war on the empire of Japan. When Robert at last turns off the radio, it is all too clear that the world they knew and loved, the tranquility they took for granted is gone. Nothing will ever be the same again.

There is no question about whether or not a healthy young man will be involved in the war. Only days later, Robert is called to go. When he tenderly kisses the tear-stained cheeks of his wife and says goodbye, he tries to reassure her. He says, "Oh Jeannie, before you know it the war will be over, and I'll rush home to you and little Questa."

Trying to be brave for his sake, she keeps her premonitions to herself. However, deep inside her there's a gnawing conviction that she'll never see him alive again. Only by a mighty inner struggle is she able to stifle the plea "Don't go! Please don't go, for if you do, you'll never come back home to me!"

At the train station that cold drizzly morning, Robert gathers his five-year-old in his arms and hugs her almost convulsively. Questa, vainly trying to push back, objects; "Daddy, you're *hurting* me!" Standing tall and ramrod straight, Robert climbs aboard the troop train. A few minutes later, mother and daughter see his face at a window and wave at him. There's a loud jolt, and another, and then, still waving, he slowly recedes from view.

* * * * *

There is no Christmas that year, for without husband and father, Jeannie and Questa find little reason to celebrate. At first his letters come regularly; then, after he ships out, only sporadically. All they know is that he is somewhere in the South Pacific. Eventually, weeks pass without any letters from him. The strain of not knowing ages Jeannie. And the war news is anything but good.

Finally, a knock on her front door. Jeannie opens the door, and there stands an unsmiling soldier with an ominous-looking

telegram in his hand. She knows, even before he speaks a word, what this means: her husband has been killed. Turns out he'd died in the fierce battle on the Bataan Peninsula in the Philippines. On that day, Jeannie's world crumbles into dust.

* * * * *

"To those who have given up, nothing seems to matter but having the days peel quickly off the calendar of life."

—Joyce Tillery Simpson

Except for Questa, Jeannie is now alone. An only child of parents who died in a diphtheria epidemic some years before and whose grandparents have all passed on as well, she now concludes that there's but one life raft left to her: Robert's widowed grandfather way up north. Since he has no telephone and mail reaches him only sporadically, she can't ask for permission to come. She decides to go anyway. After getting her affairs in order and placing most of her possessions in storage, she and Questa climb into their Ford coupe, gas up, and head north.

It is several days before she reaches her turn-off and heads toward the coast. She hopes she can find the place on her own. She's only seen it twice, and since Robert was driving, she hadn't paid much attention to landmarks along the way.

She gets lost several times on the winding dirt roads. Robert had warned her, "Don't ever attempt to get in during the rainiest season because the roads turn into quagmires."

Fortunately, the roads are dry on this day.

As she nears the coast, several times she stops and asks for directions. Then, toward evening, exhausted by *everything*, she drives up the long, steep driveway to the big, rambling house perched high above the sea, the central section of which was built of logs during pioneer days.

As her father-in-law hears Buster's raucous barking, he comes out, recognizes the Ford in spite of its thick coat of dust, and walks down the steps to bid them welcome. After hugging them, he asks Jeannie, "What have you heard lately from Robert?"

She struggles for composure before answering in a low voice: "He was killed on Bataan."

Her father-in-law's face crumples, and for some time he can't talk. Reeling, he sinks down on a stair. Time seems to have stopped.

* * * * *

Finally, awareness returns, and he shakily stands up and says, "I'm certainly not a very good host. You two must be exhausted after the long, grueling trip! Time enough to talk later. Let's bring your things in. You can have the room you and Robert" —here he winces before going on—"used during your last visit. . . . Fresh linens are in the bedroom closet. You'll want to freshen up as well.

"I'd hoped we'd have electricity brought in by now. Telephone lines too. But now there'll be no chance for that until this terrible war is over. I do my best to keep current."

"How?" she asks.

"Oh, I've rigged up a battery-powered radio contraption

that works. But the battery's running low, so I haven't used it much lately. Been waiting until my next trip to town. . . . Still, things are better than they were during your last visit. I've piped in water from the big spring high up Windy Point. The tank is full, so we aren't totally dependent any more on the well. There's a faucet on the back porch as well as one in the kitchen. Constructed a new outhouse down the hill a bit from the back door . . . After you two settle in, go ahead and clean up and take a nap. Then I'll see you in the living room. Meanwhile, I'll rustle up some grub. Later on, we'll talk."

* * * * *

Several hours later, after a welcome rest and supper, they gather in the living room. He's got a fire crackling in the great fireplace since the fog has come in from the Pacific and it has turned cold.

No one says much. As for Questa, other than her initial "Hello, Grandfather" at the car, she has not said a word. He watches her and wonders.

Finally, he clears his throat, looks at his daughter-in-law, and says, "So tell me, what are your plans?"

Even knowing this question would be coming, Jeannie is still unprepared for it. Eventually, she says, "Uh . . . Father . . . , I don't really know. We'd not saved much money, just enough to buy the car. Robert's salary paid our bills, our rent, and so on. But we have almost nothing in our saving accounts. So now, with Robert gone and no salary coming in . . . my folks dead . . . and no family to call my own—"

He breaks in, saying gently, "Say no more, dear. In other words, I'm the only person left to turn to?"

She nods her head.

There is a long silence while he digests the situation, then his face brightens with a warm smile and he says, "So you came home—which is the right place to come to. For this *is* your home—it will all be yours when I am gone. So, if you can stand the solitude and isolation, welcome *home*."

At this, Jeannie breaks into tears, tears she cannot stop. For so long has she felt dispossessed, abandoned, and destitute that just the relief of knowing she and Questa are homeless no longer is almost more than her weakened condition can handle.

Father crosses over to her, sits down next to her, puts his arm around her, and lets the weeping run its course. When she finally uses the handkerchief he's given her and dries her tears, it is growing late—confirmed by the heirloom grandfather clock sonorously bonging ten times. So he stands up and says, "Now that *that* is settled, what do you say to turning in? As for you, Questa, you can either sleep with your mother or pull out the trundle bed. See you in the morning. Go ahead and sleep in. Won't take long for the sound of the waves to lull you to sleep."

They *do* sleep in, waking up only when the morning sun drives the fog back out to sea.

After breakfast, Jeannie gives Questa permission to explore the big, three-story house, thus freeing her to divide the responsibilities with Father. She volunteers to prepare the meals, do the laundry, and keep up on all aspects of the housework, including clothes-making, thus freeing him to run his timber business, operate the ranch, plant and care for the flower garden, and maintain the fruit orchard. Questa is to help her mother as much as possible. Jeannie will be given

a budget for all her house and personal needs.

Just before they stand up, Jeannie says, "One more thing, Father. In the car trunk are Robert's cremated remains—all that is left of him. What do you think of our burying him in the little family graveyard on the knoll? Mother's already there. We should leave space for me next to him, too, when my race is run."

"I agree. I'll contact a preacher I know who lives down the coast. I'm sure he'll be willing to drive up here and conduct a graveside service when we bury Robert. *I'll* make the wooden urn. I have some walnut wood cut, milled, and dried that I've been saving for something special; I'll case it in redwood so it'll last a long time."

And so it comes to pass that in a simple but solemn service Robert is buried in the little flowering graveyard he'd tended when a child. Oh how he'd loved flowers and beauty of all kinds! He said once, "Dad, I want to make that knoll the most beautiful spot on the ranch, so even the birds will want to go there and sing! That way, it will be a happy place for all of us who go up there to remember . . . I just wish Mother had lived longer so I could have remembered her too."

The minister, who had known Robert personally, asks God to watch over this fallen soldier who gave his life for his country. And also to comfort the grieving father, wife, and daughter left behind. Now Robert has come full circle, back to the land on which he'd been born.

* * * * *

Afterwards, life settles into a routine that changes very little. Their only neighbors are Hank and Ruth, sharecroppers who had lost everything they owned during the Great Depression. They had been offered the use of a large tract of land at no cost in exchange for a promise to help on the ranch wherever and whenever needed to provide some food items—vegetables from their large vegetable garden and milk from the several cows they kept. Neither of them ever forgot the day they received that offer, for it gave them a new reason to go on living.

No professional housekeeper could have been more capable and efficient than Jeannie. As the months pass, Questa learns more and more about how to manage a house, preserve food, sew, and even quilt. But she is also given plenty of opportunity to explore the great ranch. Never does she tire of the ever-present ocean and especially the rocky coast and the occasional stretches of sandy beach.

Now it is Christmas again. Much has happened since their move to the coastal ranch. Most significant of all, however, has to do with Jeannie. Though Grandfather has done his utmost to make her happy, it is to no avail, for she has lost her glow, her joy of living. Every day she does what is required of her—does it well, but mechanically. Increasingly, Questa is left to shift for herself. On the surface, her mother continues to be all she ever was to her daughter, but where it really counts, she is not; ever so slowly, she is distancing herself further and further from her. Indeed, Jeannie even forgets her daughter's sixth birthday. It is especially obvious to the grandfather, whose heart goes out to the lonely little girl, but he dares not do anything about it lest he overstep his bounds.

Now, during the Christmas season, which had always been the most joyful time of the year, Jeannie declares she's too tired to help decorate the tree and house, too tired even

to wrap presents. As soon as the presents are passed out that Christmas Eve, she sighs audibly and says, "I'm going to bed." Then, after perfunctorily kissing her daughter on the cheek, she wearily exits the festive room.

There follows a long, awkward silence. Then, suddenly, Questa rushes across the room into her grandfather's arms, and she murmurs, "Grandfather, please hold me!" And he does, tenderly rocking her in the old family rocker that had been hauled west in a wagon train way back in the 1850s. Only the hissing, sputtering, and crackling of the fire in the fireplace breaks the silence.

Finally, Questa sits up and faces him. "Grandfather, is it always going to be like this?"

"You're referring to your mother?"

"Yes."

"Please explain what you mean by *this*."

"Oh, I don't know. It's hard to put into words. It's just . . . it's just that she's so different since . . . since Daddy died. She never laughs anymore. Never smiles either."

"She loved your father very much."

"I know that . . . but . . ."

"But what?"

"But she doesn't seem to love me . . . like she used to."

"Of *course* she loves you."

"Well, she doesn't show it. Oh, she takes good care of me. Fixes good food. Sews pretty dresses for me. But . . . that's all. We used to have such good times together. She'd sing to me—she knows ever so many songs—and I'd sing with her. We were *so* happy together. And when Daddy came into the room, we were even happier!"

"And now?"

"Now she doesn't sing at all. That's why I wonder—"

"Wonder what, dear?"

"I wonder if it'll always be like this."

The rocking continues in silence as he searches for words. Then, finally, the rocking stops, and turning her to face him, Grandfather says, "You're growing up way too fast. You've been thinking very adult thoughts. I'd hoped you'd be older before I brought up this issue, but now that you've brought it up, you and I are going to have to face it together."

"I don't understand."

"But I'm afraid you do. The truth of the matter—a truth I've delayed facing—is this: I don't know if your mother is ever again going to be like she was."

"Me, too . . . and she gets thinner and thinner."

"So you've noticed that too."

She nods her head.

"Let me put it this way: your mother is a one-man woman."

"Huh?"

"By that I mean she most likely loves only once. I have, deep down, wondered if she even wants to live without him."

"You mean, she might *die?*"

"She might—unless she wills herself to live."

"You mean to live for you . . . and me?"

"Yes, dear. Let's you and me see if we can't persuade her to become happy again—because we need her so much."

"Let's!"

* * * * *

But despite their urging her to live for their sakes, she continues to waste away, eating less and less. Barely five weeks

later, the minister returns for a second remembering service. In a handcrafted redwood casket, she is tenderly lowered into a grave next to the love of her life. The minister concludes the simple but poignant service by putting into words what everyone already knows: he says she died of a broken heart.

A new beginning

"Sorrow and joy are always twined together in life. . . . Every fresh beginning is a new birth and must have its pain as well as its joy, and without these fresh beginnings, there would be no life, without them we should turn sour like stagnant water in a pond. And always . . . the joy of a fresh beginning lures us on, outweighing the pain, dancing before us like a flame, so that hurrying to catch it the life in us keeps fresh and clear as a running stream."

—*Towers in the Mist*, by Elizabeth Goudge

That evening, rain begins to fall . . . softly at first, then in torrents, with lightning and thunder the sound effects. Inside, a man no longer young rocks a brokenhearted little girl. Finally, she murmurs, "There aren't any words, are there, Grandfather."

"No dear, at times like these there are no words."

Then, almost inaudibly, Questa asks, "Grandfather . . . ?"

"Yes?"

"I've . . . I've just been wondering . . . what will happen to me now?"

He holds her tighter before answering. "I have a suggestion."

"What is it?"

"Forgive me if I sound mixed-up, but let's see how this sounds: You no longer have either a father or a mother. I, in turn have no wife, no son, no daughter-in-law. In a way, then, we're both in the same boat. And neither of us have had any choice in the matter. So, if you're both my daughter and granddaughter all rolled into one, then I'd guess you've become the light of my life. I'll take care of you as long as I possibly can. Then you, in turn, will take care of me."

Smiling, she extends her little hand and says, "Shake, partner."

Though he laughs at her grown-up responses, he mourns the two tragedies that, in a very real way, have cut short her childhood. *She has shouldered way too much for a six-year-old,* he thinks. *Even talks and thinks like an adult. Comes from always being around adults and never being around children. Tack on that ice age of a year during which her mother froze her out of her life, leaving her with deep thoughts but with no opportunity to voice them . . . I can see I have an incredibly daunting challenge ahead of me: I must educate her, yet at the same time, see if I can help create a belated childhood for her. She certainly deserves one.*

Then, sitting up straight, he says, "Looks like this storm isn't going away tonight, so it will be mighty tough to get any sleep. We'll make up a bed for you on the couch, and I'll bunk on the floor by the fireplace, next to Buster. I'll keep the fire stoked all night so we'll stay warm no matter what—even if it snows, which rarely happens on the coast. Oh my, it's beginning to sleet now! So who knows: it *could* happen. What do you think of that?"

Yawning, she falls asleep before he can even make a bed for her.

As he tenderly looks down at the brave little girl, the last of his line, he mutters, "Life can sure play strange tricks on us."

* * * * *

By morning, the sleet has turned to snow; they now have a full-scale blizzard on their hands. The storm rages unabated for three days. Questa is entranced because it's the first snow she's ever experienced. She snuggles deeper into his arms as she watches the snow pile up outside the big window. On and off, even during daylight hours, she drops back to sleep.

Poor little tyke! She's borne enough inner trauma to last for the rest of her life. I'll just let her sleep. She'll get hungry sooner or later.

* * * * *

Spring has come at last to the Northwest coast. Grandfather asks Ruth to step in and mentor Questa in all-things-household: cooking, sewing, housecleaning, canning, preserving food in an icehouse, quilting, et cetera. Ruth is an effervescent soul who brightens up the house. And since she was never blessed with a child, there has always been an empty cavity in her heart. Thus she leaps at the opportunity to interact with Questa.

"I'd love to help!" she says. "Many are the times I've seen that forlorn little creature wandering around, looking as if she doesn't have a friend in the world! I swear, I feel ten years younger already! . . . And Hank says she's more than welcome to help with the milking and vegetable gardening."

* * * * *

Early one May morning after the chores are done, Grandfather and Questa walk up the familiar path to the knoll. There, flowers are already starting to bloom. They sit down on one of the hand-hewn benches, look out at the retreating fog, and listen to the sea birds.

After a while, Grandfather says, "Questa, since you and I are bestest of friends, I'd like our chat this morning to serve as a bridge to our tomorrows. Let's see if I can't bring even more happiness into your life."

"But Grandfather, you already *have!*"

"Well, thank you, but I intend to make you even happier. To get to know you better, I'm going to ask you a series of questions, and then you can ask *me* questions. Sound OK?"

"Yes."

"All right. First question: what do you like best about the ranch?"

"That's easy. The ocean. I love listening to it, watching it. It's always different. I love walking along the shore with Buster. Why, here he comes now! Come here, Buster." And she scratches his ears.

"Next question. I know you've thoroughly explored the house. Which part of it do you like best?"

"Oh, several parts of it. The living room—especially the fireplace. The big kitchen stove. It kinda comforts me when I'm cold. The library, of course. But most of all, my favoritest—is there such a word?—part of all is the tower. But I've always wondered what it's for."

"Now that's an interesting story. Back in the 1850s, when our ancestors came west to this part of the country, this was a dangerous place. Indians who'd been mistreated were not always friendly. There was no government then to protect us against people who wished us no good, so we had to protect *ourselves*. Even today, life is not completely safe. That's why I tell you to always keep Buster by your side when you're away from our compound. At a hundred and twenty pounds, not many are likely to mess with him."

"But the *tower*, Grandfather."

"Oh yes, the tower. It was constructed as part of the original log portion of the house, which was as much a fort as a dwelling place. In case of attack, the lower windows could be shuttered, and the doors barred. And the tower itself—well, you could see everything, everyone, from there."

"That's why I like it. I like to just sit there and look out . . . and think. I like to read there too. I can be my own person up there."

"I like the way you put that. It's . . . it's a lifelong struggle, being your own person, because so many other people want to be part of us too. That can make life very complicated sometimes. But you're right, Questa, the core of who you are, of who I am, is always a very special place. One that can be either a heaven or a hell."

"I don't understand."

"Well, let's see if I can explain. You see, as I pointed out in worship the other day, there are two powers in the world who fight to control, to possess, us—the dark power in a negative way. He wants to *own* us. Not God. He wants us to be His, but He doesn't want to own us, but rather wants us to keep sacred the core—the soul—He created in us."

"That's . . . uh . . . deep, Grandfather."

"Yes, it is. But let me simplify: Whatever you think changes you. Whatever you read changes you. Same for what you see and hear. *Everything* changes you. Never stops. Even at my age."

"At *your* age?"

"Yes," he says, smiling, "at my age. For instance, now that you are a part of my life, every day that I am around you, I change because you enrich my life, make it much more interesting than it was when I was all alone. But because I love you so much, I sometimes worry about you too."

"Why?"

"Because right now life may seem fairly simple. It's just us on this isolated ranch. But it won't always be so. You will grow up, the good Lord willing, and other people will come into your life—some good, some bad. It will sometimes be difficult to know the truth about people. And then there's—"

"There's *what*, Grandfather?"

"Well, your mother was a very beautiful woman."

"I know that."

"Well, she could all too easily have married the wrong man—most beautiful women do just that, and they suffer for it the rest of their lives. Your mother was lucky. She married my son, Robert, who was always, even when your age, his own person. And even then, he knew what kind of a person he wanted to spend the rest of his life with."

"So how did he meet her?"

"Your mother? Now, that's an interesting story. It was at a camp meeting."

"A camp meeting? What's that?"

"Oh, it's a gathering of church people where they talk about God and His leading in their lives. Young people get together there and sing, listen to stories, have fun. . . .

"Well, at one particular camp meeting, Robert couldn't help noticing a lovely girl who couldn't help noticing him. Their eyes met, and they had trouble disengaging. It's interesting; sometimes there *is* such a thing as love at first sight. At any rate, we had tried to instill in him the concept that though outer beauty might be nice to look at, it won't last. Only inner beauty can.

"Well, your father discovered that your mother was just as beautiful inside as she was outside. And God was central to her. Robert told us, after that camp meeting, that they had promised to write each other. He told me, and he was only fourteen at the time, 'I'm going to marry that girl, Daddy!' And eight years later, he did."

"Grandfather, I can't remember much about Daddy. I want you to tell me more stories about him."

"I will, but now it's your turn. It's time for you to choose a bedroom for yourself. Which room do you want?"

"The tower."

"Away up there?"

"Yes. I can be my own person there."

"We'll see what we can do about that. What else would you like to do, to have as just your own?"

"I'd like to take care of the knoll all by myself . . . just like Daddy did."

"It's yours. Anything else?"

"Well, . . . yes. I love to read, but your library . . . it's big."

"It ought to be—we've been adding to it for close to a hundred years."

"But it's a library for old people, not much for little girls like me."

"Well, I'll be! Guess you're right about that. You've given

me work to do. I'll get together with Hank later this morning, and we'll make plans for your room. And as for the library, I'll do something about that too."

"Grandfather?"

"Yes, dear."

"I love you awfully much!"

Questa turns seven

> Come, let us kiss you, Newly Seven,
> Seven times and once to grow on,
> For the new year may not go on
> Till the lucky kiss be given,
> Child of Heaven, newly seven.
>
> Your eyes, so confidently blue,
> They were your mother's eyes before you,
> And the gay spirit looking through,
> It was the mother's soul that bore you;
> Therefore, Seven, we adore you.
>
> Her beauty was the gift of Heaven,
> And yours, child, too, is godly-given,
> For it doth seem to me that even
> Thus Jesus looked when He was seven.
>
> —"To a Little Child," by Gouverneur Morris

Her seventh birthday! What a festive occasion it has been! Hank and Ruth were invited to attend too. Of course, Questa never called them by their first names; it just wasn't proper for a

child to do such things! To her, they were always "Uncle Hank" and "Aunt Ruth"—indeed, they were the only uncle and aunt she had. Aunt Ruth had even baked her a special cake.

But now, the shadows of evening have fallen and grandfather and granddaughter are alone together, not talking, just dreaming. Suddenly, she breaks the silence. "Grandfather?"

"Yes, dear?"

"Today, Aunt Ruth asked me a question I couldn't answer: She asked, 'How did you get the name *Questa*? You're the only person I've ever met with that name!' Do *you* know, Grandfather?"

Smiling, he leans back in his favorite armchair and, with a faraway look in his eyes, says, "I've been wondering when you'd ask that question.

"You were born in the city. Your parents moved there after they were married. Your father told me, 'Dad, I want to be a man and stand on my own two feet. I have a good job offer, so Jeannie and I have decided I should accept it. Someday, when you really need me, I'll come home and help you with the ranch—but not right now.'

"It was just about a year after their marriage that you were born. As your due date neared, your father wrote me asking if I could possibly be there when you were born. For me, it was a long, hard trip out, so I just barely made it. A neighborhood woman was kind enough to help out. She remained there all through your birth. You evidently weren't in any hurry to be born, so we all had quite a wait. Your father tenderly held your mother's hand all through the process, wincing each time she moaned, wiping away the sweat on her face, and urging her to just be strong a little longer.

"Finally, after what seemed to all of us to be an eternity,

you emerged. I wish you could have seen your mother's pain-wracked face. Weakened though she was, when she cradled you in her arms, her face was beautified with sacred love. She was like a biblical Madonna. She just kept kissing you and hugging you."

"Oh! Oh!"

"Why 'Oh'?"

"It's because . . . because, after Daddy died, Mommy . . . uh . . . didn't seem like she loved me anymore. I've always wondered what awful thing I must have done—because she seemed so far away. I didn't really know if she wanted me around anymore."

"Questa, you mustn't ever doubt your mother's love for you. Love is such a complex, mysterious thing. No one can explain it. Your mother just loved your father so much that when he died, she died too. Indeed, it *was* a sort of death because it took away the glow her face had retained ever since your father first told her he loved her. His adoration for her every day of their married life was so constant that the glow on her face never went away. When he walked into the room, she'd look at him, and the look in her eyes was all but blinding.

"But let me share a scene with you. I was going to wait until you were a little older to do it, but I can't think of a better time to do it than now.

"It was during the last night of your mother's life. All evening long she'd been unresponsive. I could tell she was sinking and that the end of her journey was near. Then something happened—one of those strange phenomena that sometimes happen just before a person passes away. At about two o'clock in the morning she suddenly roused herself, sat up, and cried out. No, it was far more than a mere cry; it was an agonized

wail! Gone now was that glazed look that had clouded her eyes ever since your father died. In its place was the old radiance. It was like she suddenly awoke out of a long trance and realized for the very first time an awful truth about herself and her behavior. So . . . clutching my arm all the time, she, in a brokenhearted voice, wailed, 'Oh, Father! — I've been so cold to Questa! She must think I don't love her anymore! Oh, Father, I do! I do! It's just that with Robert gone, life for me was just not worth living. *Oh Father! Oh Father!* Please . . . please . . . *please* tell her for me how *very much* I love her . . . how very . . . much . . .' and the light in her eyes that almost blinded me faded, and she was gone. Those were her last words."

* * * * *

There follows the most tempestuous, unrestrained weeping of Questa's life. She crawls like a wounded animal into her grandfather's lap, curls up into a fetal position, and almost convulsively sobs. It is as though somewhere deep inside her a dam has buckled. For so long have the waters of her past backed up behind the dam of her mother's coldness and death, compounded by the earlier death of her father, that now Grandfather's story detonates—with all the power of a massive bomb—the dam that has held back the full flowering of her childhood. For several hours the turgid waters of the last couple of years thunder through her and down the canyons of her past, never to return. Wisely, not once during the cleansing flood has he said a word—he just holds her, once in a while kissing her all but furrowed head. Even then, words are not necessary, their two hearts being that much in tune with each other.

Finally, after a deep sigh, awareness returns—and with it a mischievous smile: "Grandfather, you *still* haven't told me how I got my name."

"Guess I didn't. Sorry. It was this way: For a long time your parents had been discussing possible names for you. Both boy and girl names since they didn't know until you emerged which one you'd be. Your father kept saying, 'I hope it's a girl who'll grow up to be as lovely as her mother.' "

Shivering ecstatically, Questa sings out, "Daddy loved me too, then, didn't he!"

"How could you ever have doubted that? From the moment you were born, he was your slave. You knew instinctively: all girls do—they don't need psychology classes to teach them that—how to coerce him into doing your will. All you had to do was look up at him with tears in your eyes, and he'd come unglued. Needless to say, he had a terrible time disciplining you. Your mother would roguishly wag her finger and lecture him: 'You're just a big softy! You'll ruin her!' "

"And—how did I get my name?"

"Give me time. Your mother was in such a weakened state after you were born that your father hired a nurse from the city. Lucy Montemayór was her name. She was there for three months before your mother fully regained her strength."

"But Grandfather!"

"I am a tad slow at getting to it, aren't I. Anyway, Lucy was captivated by you from the very first day. Said your eyes were too knowing for a baby's. That 'they looked at me as though she could read me like a book'—her very words. Your mother didn't help much in naming you—she was far too weak. So your dad, Lucy, and I were the only ones in the voting loop.

"One day, several weeks after you were born, Lucy said, 'I'm going to put my prophetic hat on and make a prediction: This baby is going to grow up into a woman who will have an insatiable desire to learn everything in the world there is to know. Life, for her, is going to be one continuous quest for knowledge.'

"Your dad broke in, in that decisive way he had, saying, 'You've got it! I've also seen that sometimes faraway look in her eyes and thought: *I wonder what she's thinking—I'll bet they aren't baby thoughts.* What do you think of naming her "Questa"? Because for her, life is going to be one long and grand quest.'"

"And Questa you've been from that day to this."

* * *

No sooner have these last words left his mouth than Questa looks up at him with eyes that have been reborn. It's almost as though every time he's looked into her eyes before, there was an almost imperceptible shadow in them; something dimming the wattage. But now, for the first time since her father's passing, the radiance in her eyes almost blinds him. *Questa has her mother's eyes!*

* * * * *

The summer sun is fair today
Upon the sandy beach;
The sails are white upon the bay
As far as eye can reach.

With pail and shovel here we build
Frail houses out of sand,
Forgetting that the restless tide
Is creeping up the strand.

We build and still we build, and then
Alas for our array!
A wave runs higher than the rest
And sweeps them all away.

A brief lament, then farther back
We fashion them once more,
Till once again the wave comes in
And takes them as before.

Dear little heart, through life we build
Frail houses out of sand,
And watch the tide of years roll in
And sweep them from the strand;

Yet keep on building day by day,
Still higher up the beach,
While hope sails white across the bay
As far as eye can reach.

—"Sand Houses," by Albert Bigelow Paine

Whenever work and study are over, it is rare when Questa cannot be found with Buster, at one with the breakers rolling in to shore, reveling in all the multitudinous sights, smells, sounds, and sensations of the ever-changing sea. Whether calm or stormy, turbulent or serene, they exult in whatever weather God brings their way.

Sometimes it would be climbing up and down and round the glistening rocks, and just as often they'd be wandering down the sandy beaches, searching for seashells, sand dollars, agates, or castaway things from who knows where.

And how they love to build sandcastles, the larger the better. Buster, of course, would just dig for the joy of digging, tunnel down to unearth a crab; or perhaps chase down a sandpiper or seagull, certain that this time he'd finally catch one, and yet never be discouraged when they'd fly away.

* * * * *

Questa's real education begins the day the radiance comes back into her eyes. Indeed, it proves to be the turning point of her life. Before then, she dutifully followed orders, doing what she was told. Now, however, Lucy's long-ago prophecy comes true: so excited is she about every moment of every day; that she it is who, more often than not, now takes the initiative: machine-gunning questions at poor Grandfather at such a rate that he sometimes begs for mercy!

Grandfather is a true Renaissance man, and his expanding library testifies of this. For years, however, all he'd lacked was an audience. Gifted with a marvelous memory, he knows entire plays such as Shakespeare's *Hamlet* by heart. One evening, when he thought she was in bed, she slipped down for a drink of water and caught him in midperformance, thundering out his lines. Mesmerized, she stopped, stunned by his ability to bring fictional people to life. She'd never realized he had it in him. It didn't take her long to discover he was also a voracious reader of biographies and literature, be it full-length books or short stories. History and art as well. And how he loved to recite poetry! Especially the likes of Tennyson, Longfellow, Kipling, Frost, Wordsworth, Yeats, Browning—oh, the list could go on and on! The result is that Grandfather becomes her school, academy, college, and university, all rolled into one. There are no bells ringing to begin or conclude classes; with him and with Questa, class is *always* in session.

* * * * *

It is late June before Grandfather and Hank are able to

seriously tackle the remodeling of the tower. Questa is ordered to stay away until the job is done. The hammering and sawing and moving lumber, hardware, and glass in and out keep her curiosity at fever pitch. Hank had driven the truck into town in order to get items not available on the ranch. Ruth had gone with him in search of bedding, curtains, pictures, and other things she felt a girl like Questa would be drawn to.

Now, the great day arrives at last! A broad length of ribbon is stretched across the doorway to her new room. Questa is first blindfolded, then led upstairs into the doorway; when the blindfold is removed, she gasps. Here is the room of her dreams! Aunt Ruth had somehow managed to take Questa's sketchy wish list and create with it a real work of art. There is even a fireplace, made possible because the chimney runs up one side of the tower. And, surprise of all surprises, the men had attached a balcony to the seaside part of the room! From it, she could bask in the sun, read, dream, look out to sea.

She is literally speechless, so she settles on the next best thing: running up to, first, Uncle Hank; second, Aunt Ruth; and finally, Grandfather, giving each a strangling hug.

Then they silently slip away, close her door, and she is alone like a storybook princess, imprisoned high in a castle tower. She opens the door to the balcony veranda, leans over the railing, and murmurs, "Can heaven be greater than this?"

* * * * *

Next morning early, Grandfather knocks on her door. When she sleepily asks, "Who is it?" he responds. "It's Grandfather. Quick, get up, wash up, put on your clothes, and meet me at the car in twenty minutes. We're going to town, and we'll eat there."

Going to town is always exciting, for she gets to do it so rarely. Dawn is just breaking as she climbs into the car, and they reach town about 9:30. After breakfast in the Sunshine Cafe, Grandfather's all-time favorite breakfast spot, he moves on to the county library. It's Questa's first time to enter a library other than Grandfather's. But he knows the head librarian well. After some small talk, he explains to her why they're here. His seven-year-old granddaughter, Questa, loves reading, but his library at home contains very few books for children. So they're here to get counsel. Grandfather asks if she would be willing to give Questa a tour of the library, pointing out to her which books and authors girls like her consider most interesting.

The genial librarian smiles. "Of course! Come along, Questa, and I'll give you the grand tour. As we go along, if you see any book you'd like to read, you can put it in one of our carts. Later on, when we're all done, we'll make up a library card for you. Then we'll check out all the books you choose, and you can take them home with you. Ordinarily, all books are due back in two weeks, but since your ranch is so far away, we'll give you two months. If you need more time, we can re-check them then. So here's a cart; let's be on our way."

Grandfather pipes in, "I'll be the horse pulling the cart; and, as you talk to Questa, I'll be writing author names and book titles down. We'll need them because after we leave you, our next stop is the bookstore. While we're there, I'll be helping Questa to choose some books for her own library."

* * * * *

By noon, Questa has checked out a large box of books.

The real fun begins at the bookstore, for *these* books will be her *very own!* It is midafternoon before they finish there. They haul three boxes of books to the car and put them in the trunk. Then they get in themselves, and Grandfather announces, "We'll go to just one more place." Shortly afterward, they stop in front of a building sporting a sign on the front door that says this building is an animal shelter.

Upon entering, Grandfather asks the receptionist if anyone has brought in any kittens or cats lately. The receptionist groans, " 'If *anyone* . . . !' If you only knew how many lonely, unwanted animals are here waiting for a loving heart to rescue them and give them a home!"

Questa breaks in. "Kittens? You have kittens? More than one?"

"Yes indeed, Miss. We have at least a dozen. Want to see them?"

She leads Questa to a large cage in which kittens of various sizes, colors, and breeds lay resignedly in their cramped quarters. Carefully and intently, she studies each one. A stunning shaded-silver Persian stands out.

Noticing Questa's interest in it, the receptionist says, "That one won't be here long. Came in yesterday. Its owner moved in a hurry and left her behind. You'd *love* that one. *So* beautiful!"

But Questa isn't ready to choose just yet. After taking her time petting each one, she returns to an emaciated black and white angora with matted fur.

The receptionist explains why it's in this condition: "A fisherman brought her in just this morning. Said he'd seen a man heave something in a gunny sack off a bridge. Suspicious as to what might be in it, the fisherman dropped his rod, dived into the creek, and reached the sack just as it was sinking out of sight. When he reached the shore and opened the sack, he found this bedraggled kitten, more dead than alive. He thought, *Poor little thing! Looks like she's all but starved. Hardly any flesh on her bones. Can't imagine anyone wanting her, but I want to give her a chance at life anyway.* So he brought her in."

Questa tenderly picks her up. She is *so* tiny! Just skin and bones. So unlovely to look at. The eyes of the little kitten look up into Questa's, and she struggles to snuggle deeper into Questa's arms. Then ever so faintly she begins to purr, and her little pink tongue reaches out to lick Questa's right thumb.

With an air of decision, Questa turns to Grandfather and says, "This is the one I want. She needs me most."

The receptionist turns to Grandfather and warns, "Sir, I hate to release this kitten in its current condition. She is so weak and malnourished it will be a miracle if she lives."

Noting the look in Questa's eyes, Grandfather responds decisively: "No, it's this one or none. My granddaughter has chosen. Perhaps love will pull the kitten through."

A struggle it certainly turns out to be: for days the kitten hovers between life and death. But Questa nurses her, attempts to feed her, and holds her to her heart through several days and nights, refusing to give in. Finally, on the fourth day, Questa wins out: the kitten will live. Then, completely exhausted, Questa falls asleep and doesn't awaken until the following day.

A full week passes before Questa can settle on a name. Then she explains her dilemma to Grandfather: "The only name for her that's just right is 'Lazarus,' because she was raised from the dead just like him. But Lazarus was a man, and this is a girl-kitty. What should I do?"

In response her grandfather says, "What if you called her Lazara—Laza for short?"

"Perfect! I knew you'd help me, Grandfather!"

And so Laza is bathed and combed and brushed and fed so assiduously that it isn't very long before she blossoms into adorable kittenhood. Laza mourns whenever Questa goes anywhere without her. She wails nonstop, refusing to be comforted, until Questa returns. But to tell the truth, Questa needs that love as much as Laza does, for it helps to fill the void left in her heart by the passing of her mother and father.

Buster, on the other hand, is most confused by this Lilliputian intruder into his kingdom. When he tries to investigate, Laza swells up to twice her size, glares, spits, and attempts to claw him. Finally, he just moves any time Laza comes close. But that doesn't work either, for Laza follows him and even jumps up on his back pretending he's her elephant. The look in his eyes is one of sheer martyrdom. The final straw comes when Laza plops herself down between his big paws, begins to purr, and falls asleep against him. At that, he does the wise thing: he surrenders.

The coming of a journal

> He who gives a child a book,
> Gives that child a sweeping look,
> Through its pages
> Down the ages.
>
> Gives that child a ship to sail,
> Where the far adventurers hail
> Down the sea
> Of destiny.

> Gives that child great dreams to dream;
> Sunlit days that glint and gleam
> Where the sages
> Tramp the ages.

—"The Child and the Book," by William L. Stidger

Questa's eighth and ninth years turn out to be a magical time, for she has discovered books. Grandfather's regular trips to the bookstore have changed the complexion of her tower room. Fortunately, the room was so large to begin with that part of it was partitioned off. Now it's clear that, at the rate her library is expanding, it will soon be necessary to move the partition back.

Questa never has need to be lonely now, for her inner world is rapidly being filled with "live" people discovered in her books: characters such as Spyri's Heidi, Tarkington's Penrod, Gene Stratton-Porter's Freckles, and Eleanor Porter's Pollyanna. Grandfather even acquires a complete run (1873–1939) of the greatest children's magazine ever printed—*St. Nicholas* (more than seventy thousand pages of reading)—that provides endless delight to the bookworm high up in her tower.

And then there's that very special present on the occasion of her eighth birthday: a beautiful book. But upon opening the book, Questa's face falls. "But Grandfather," she says, "all the pages are blank!"

"True, my dear. It's called a journal . . . or a diary."

"What's it for?"

"Well, every day new experiences come your way—some sad and some happy. Life is full of both. You will meet new people, such as the ones you've already met in church. Then

there are the people you meet in books, in magazines, in poems. Let's say you're reading *Heidi*—is not Clara real to you? Even without the illustrations in the book, as you read, you create mental pictures of the characters."

"So how does all that get written in my journal?"

Laughing, Grandfather responds, "Never fear, it doesn't—only some of it. Let's see . . . Oh, I know. You have no brother or sister to talk with. Why not create one? Perhaps a book character you feel is so real that you think, 'Oh, how I wish Anne was my sister! What great times we'd have together! We'd talk half the night away.' "

"You mean, like Anne of Green Gables?"

"It could be. Or it could be a person you could create in your own mind. Give her a special name. Pretend she's real. Then, each time you open your journal to write about that day's experiences, you could address it to your imaginary sister and tell her all your most intimate thoughts—things you wouldn't say even to me."

"Grandpa! And you wouldn't peek?"

"Cross my heart: I won't peek."

"So, how could I tell her everything? I'd be writing all day."

"You can't. It would be impossible. You write about only the special things that are really meaningful to you. And you don't want to fill the pages with 'I did this and that today.' You'd soon tire of reading your diary—it would bore you. Instead, pick up on something you consider special and relate it to something or someone you cherish. For instance, of all Alcott's characters, who do you relate to most?"

"That's easy: Jo."

"Why?"

"Oh, I don't know . . . Perhaps because she's always goofing up, making mistakes . . . making new friends. She's adventuresome; I never know what she's going to do next. She loves books and acting in plays."

"So if Jo were a close friend in real life, would you enjoy writing to her?"

"Would I! I'd love to."

"What would you tell her? Things you've done, people you know, mistakes you've made, book passages you've read that make you think of similar things or people in Jo's life. Wouldn't you have plenty to write about?"

"I'm afraid I'd ramble on and on. . . . But I'm curious. Why is it important that I write at all? Isn't it enough that I just *think* it?"

"No, it's not."

"Why?"

"Let's see. I know you love the poetry of Emily Dickinson. Tell me why."

"Because . . . she . . . uh . . . she makes me think."

"I agree. Let me quote one of my favorite Dickinson poems:

"Your thoughts don't have words every day
They come a single time
Like signal esoteric sips
Of the communion Wine
Which while you taste so native seems
So easy so to be
You cannot comprehend its price
Nor its infrequency.

"Now let me rephrase it in words you understand better. Emily declares that we're given each thought we have only once in life. Each one comes like a single sip of Communion wine. And as you taste it, it seems so natural, even so common, that we can easily take it for granted, so that you don't really value it much; nor do you realize how rare each one actually is. *Now*, out of all Dickinson says, what part of it do you feel relates best to the importance of journal writing?"

"Well, . . . I think it's that we're given each thought only once, and if we don't write it down *immediately*, we'll lose it because it won't ever come again."

"Bravo! This doesn't mean that God doesn't give us similar thoughts later on, but never again in the exact phraseology of an earlier one.

"So, here's another question: Have you ever had a thought that really rang bells in your mind; one that made you say to yourself, 'I really ought to write that down, but I'm tired, so I'll write it down tomorrow.' Tell me, come next morning, is it still there?"

"Well, maybe, but it's like mush. It doesn't sing anymore."

"Exactly. That's why you write special things in your journal each day. That way, all the rest of your life, when you want to relive a special experience or see how you reacted to a special event, you'll be able to retrieve from in your journals."

"But won't I think wise thoughts—like yours—when I get older? Won't I think then, *Oh, that is so simple. I was just a child when I wrote that?*"

"True. You'll do just that. But when you get older, you will lose the ability to think like an eight-year-old girl. So someday in the future, when you have an eight-year-old girl of your very own, you can show her the thoughts you wrote when you were eight. What will she say then?"

Chuckling, Questa responds, "She'll say, 'Mommy, why, you used to be a little girl just like me!' "

"So, my dear, keeping a journal all your life long will enable you to preserve each step of your life's journey—all that is most important. So, in later years, when you become a writer like Alcott, Montgomery, Austen, or Dickinson, you'll be able to look back through your journals and incorporate them into your own books. And I predict, your voice will be needed."

"Oh, Grandfather, you say that just because you love me."

"Partly. But it's also because I think you *will* be a writer."

"All right, Grandfather. I can hardly wait to write in my journal. I'm going to call my new dearest friend *Anne*."

* * * * *

Such conversations with her grandfather fill most every day of Questa's life, and as a result, her mind continues to expand. He makes her *think*! Think for herself. Makes her search in the dictionary for not just a possible word for something, but for the *perfect* word. Thus both the unabridged dictionary and *Roget's Thesaurus* are always being consulted when she's searching for the right word to use in a sentence. And she'd learned long before that Grandfather tolerates no sloppiness or laziness in her sentence and paragraph construction. In fact, even before she turned eight she'd graduated to the understanding and use of colons, semicolons, hyphens, dashes, and ellipses.

The same is true for knowledge in general. There are several encyclopedia sets in the library, one for young people. That one she reads a *lot*, like a storybook. The *Britannica* she

consults when she wants to dig deeper into something.

Grandfather's approach to grammar is to steer clear of long lists of grammatical rules, except for reference purposes. Instead, he prefers that she read widely from authors whose works have stood the test of time: "Questa," he says, "each author has a style of writing uniquely his or her own. The more styles you have in your head to draw from, the more options you'll have to draw from when you write—and your writing will be the richer for it."

Grandfather is a tough but fair critic. When Questa has completed the writing assignments he's given her, he examines them to ensure that they are clear, concise, persuasive, and interesting: "Questa, if the first sentence, the first paragraph, of what you write doesn't suck your reader in, what then? I'll let you answer that."

After thinking for a moment, she says, "If the first sentence or paragraph doesn't make my reader want to read on: to find out what other interesting things I might say, then . . . , then . . . , why am I writing in the first place? Is it all just for *me*?"

"That's precisely the point. And even if it *is* just for you, if you can't interest yourself, believe me, you'll soon heave the essay, poem, or story into the wastebasket.

"Furthermore, why is it that whenever in your reading you find a fresh, original metaphor or simile, I require you to stop and write it down at the back of your journal?"

"I'm guessing that it's not for me to copy it and use it in my own writing, because that would be lazy of me. Using someone else's originality wouldn't make *me* an original writer. You just want me to be more conscious of the power of creating my own unique metaphors and similes."

"Exactly! Now let's get back to those beginning sentences and paragraphs that make it very hard for you to quit reading. I want you to stop everything else and rummage around in your favorite books until you find just such a beginning. Then bring it to me, and we'll look it over."

* * * * *

"So you found one?"

"Yes, Grandfather—the beginning of Louisa May Alcott's *Little Women*."

"OK; let's hear it."

"Christmas won't be Christmas without any presents," grumbled Jo, lying on the rug.

"It's so dreadful to be poor," sighed Meg, looking down at her old dress.

"I don't think it's fair for some girls to have plenty of pretty things, and other girls nothing at all," added little Amy with an injured sniff.

"We've got Father and Mother and each other," said Beth contentedly from her corner.

"Excellent," responds Grandfather. "That beginning would certainly make *me* want to read the book. But can you think of another reason Alcott might have chosen those four beginning sentences?"

After thinking a moment or two, she gingerly suggests, "Might it be because each girl's sentence reflects her entire personality—what sets her apart from her sisters? I even suspect Alcott may have written that paragraph *after* she finished

the entire book—they match so perfectly."

Grandfather smiles beatifically: "You know, I think I'm going to keep you."

Grandmother

The thirtieth day of May, 1946, has arrived, and Questa has just turned ten. Much has happened during the last year. What is now being called World War II has finally ended. With it, at last, what we call "progress" is significantly affecting her life. Electric power and telephone lines reach the ranch. What dramatic changes have resulted!

"Well, young lady, are you overwhelmed with all the changes?"

"*Overwhelmed* is certainly the right word for it, Grandfather. No more outhouses. No more wasps and flies. How I hated to go there when it was raining or bitterly cold outside. What a joy when bathrooms were put in! Never again that big copper tub we'd take turns using; so no more having to heat all those kettles of water in the fireplace or on the woodstove.

"As for the kitchen, what a relief to no longer have to cook on the woodstove or in the fireplace. The kitchen would often get so hot it was like a furnace in there! Now food can be preserved in the refrigerator, so we don't have to go down to the icehouse anymore.

"And I like playing records on a record player instead of winding up the old Victrola. I listen to the radio programs more too."

"So, Questa, is there anything you miss from what we'll now call 'the olden days?' "

"Yes, never thought I'd admit it, though. It's nice having electric lights, but they're so glary! I find myself missing the softer light so much that in the evening, when I read in my room, I often light candles or the kerosene lamps rather than turn on those bright room lights.

"And I don't quite know how to respond to that telephone box hanging on the wall. Odd-looking contraption. I find myself both loving it and loathing it—and a lot in between."

"How's that?"

"Oh, I love it because it opens up the whole world to us. That is, if we could afford those terribly expensive long-distance calls. But I loathe it because it destroys the quiet, serene life we had before. Impossible to ignore it, as those rings could wake the dead!"

"And 'in-between'?"

"Well, I find it funny because, since we're on a party line, when I lift the receiver, I no sooner start talking than one after another I hear *click, click, click* as our neighbors pick up their receivers in order to listen in—so, we have no privacy at all!"

"I'm so glad you'd never do such a thing, Questa."

"Grandfather, I think you're being a tad sarcastic. I must confess that when the telephone rings four times, I know it's for crotchety old Mrs. Partridge, who everlastingly gets everyone riled up because she gossips about all of us. I'm always curious about who in the world would call her! And I'm *tempted* to listen in. Not that I do—usually, that is. But even so, Grandfather, I do like the modern age."

* * * * *

After a long silence, Questa asks a question she's wondered about for many years. "Grandfather, are we rich?"

"Rich? Not necessarily. Before the Depression hit, our

family was what I'd call well-to-do, but after it hit 'way back in 1929, hard times—terribly hard times—came to us all. And things stayed bad a long, long time. Only now that the war has finally come to an end have things started looking up."

"Grandfather, you get lots of mail. Men often come to see you, and you write on documents they hand you. I hear you on the telephone talking to them. So I've just been wondering—"

"Wondering what I do for a living?"

She nods her head.

"It's this way. Our family wealth has been in timber for a very long time. In other words, in growing trees—lots and lots of trees. When lumber is needed for building houses, the lumbermen come to me, and I tell them which of our trees they can cut down."

"I see trees here, but I don't see anyone cutting them down."

"Oh, most of those are some distance from here: most are in Oregon, Washington, and British Columbia."

"Sounds like a lot!"

"It *is*. Lots to pay taxes on. That's why we've been timber-rich and money-poor for a very long time."

"You've told me a lot about President Teddy Roosevelt and how he saved so many millions of acres of national park land for the American people. So I wonder, have we helped conserve forests—or do we just cut them down, leaving ugly stumps?"

"I was hoping you'd bring this up as you grew older. Yes, we have practiced conservation, and we continue to do so. Even before Teddy Roosevelt came along, your ancestors were so horrified by the mass destruction of our forests, lakes, and streams that they decided to do something about it. They preserved as much old-growth forest as they could. Second, they set aside large sections of forest to remain wild so that a century later these trees, too, could become old growth. The rest they harvested by the mode they called selectively cut rather than clear-cut. Selectively cut timber is less lucrative because it's much cheaper to clear-cut. And that, my dear, is why we've been timber-rich and money-poor so much of the time. By the way, we've contributed large stands of old-growth timber to the National Park Service so they'd be preserved forever."

"I'm so glad to hear all this, Grandfather. I'd want to carry on that tradition."

"Good! Any more questions?"

"Yes. . . . I see pictures of Grandma in the house. Whatever happened to her?"

Pain etches its way across his face, and he struggles for composure. Then, finally, he says, "Forgive me, dear. . . . It's just that it still hurts terribly—even after so many years have passed."

"Yet you never talk about her."

"No, but it's not because I don't think about her, for she haunts this house still. For so many years growing up and during our courtship, she was in my thoughts and dreams night and day. I really had to fight to get her."

"Why?"

"Because she was the prettiest girl in three counties. Believe me, I had a *lot* of competition!"

"Yet she chose you."

"Yes, even though she was way too good for me. One day, on a walk, when I proposed for the third time, a tender look

came into her eyes as she admitted she'd *always* loved me—even when she was eight and I was ten."

"So why didn't she say Yes the first time you proposed?"

"Because she felt that if I'd won her too easily, I wouldn't value her as much."

"Oh."

"Anyway, ours was a fairy-tale romance. We loved each other just as intensely as your parents loved each other. About two years into our marriage, it became clear that she was pregnant. We were both ecstatic: a child at last! And then Bobby was born."

"My daddy?"

"Yes. He was born in this house, and he was all we hoped he'd be. A beautiful baby. Your grandmother was so happy she couldn't stop smiling. Especially happy since she so longed for a son."

"So what happened, Grandfather?"

"The doctors called it 'childbirth complications' back then. Lots of mothers died from it. In my bride's case, instead of regaining her strength after your father was born, she grew weaker and weaker, no small thanks to a persistent fever. Then, one dreadful

night—" Unconsciously, Questa takes his arm, and while he struggles for control she leans her head against his shoulder, saying nothing.

"It was just before dawn one morning when the end came. We both knew it was coming but were powerless to stop it. We had so many plans for the wonderful life we would share. Oh, a lifetime was far too short a time for all we wanted to do together!

"As she began to sink into that final sleep, she roused one last time. It was as if she realized she only had energy left for a few last words—and she had to make each one count. First of all, she grieved that now I'd have to be both father *and* mother to little Bobby. And second, she worried that her passing would wreck all the life plans we'd made. So, she did make those few words count. She said, 'Love him for me' and 'Oh darling, how can I leave you!' "

He can say no more.

It is some time before he can regain his composure. . . . Eventually, he says, "Then she was gone. The light of my life. As you know, she's buried near your father and mother on top of the knoll. Promise me you'll place me next to her when I go."

Incapable of speech, she can only nod.

"I've told you that memories of her never leave me. Everywhere I turn there are things she loved that remind me of her. Often I dream about her at night. Her clear, loving eyes looking at me—how I hate to wake up! Rather than explain further what it's like to live without her, I'm going to recite an old poem that describes what it's like. I memorized it long ago:

"How crowded now these empty rooms
Have grown since she is gone—

No trifle but becomes a thing
That thought must wait upon!

"The very silence seems to move
About on stealthy feet,
Tiptoeing lest it wake some thought
The heart would dread to meet.

"And oh, the leaden sense of all
Irrevocable fate
In that neglected glove still left
So close beside its mate!"

—"Absence," by Melville Upton

But then, with an uplift in his voice, he adds, "But I know I'll see her in the kingdom!"

"Oh, Grandfather!"

It is some time before he smiles through his tears and says, "And now she is gone, your father is gone, your mother is gone—all I have left is *you.*"

Her response is so muffled he has to bend close to hear her: "And all *I* have left is *you.*"

* * * * *

Never after that memorable day has Questa been able to think of her grandfather merely as the person who makes her day-to-day life possible. Now she realizes that though he is old, deep inside him are wounds that rival her own. On this day *empathy* ceases to be an abstract word for her.

Letters

It is a cold drizzly day, this day after her twelfth birthday. Grandfather has the sniffles, so Questa is left without an assignment. But he has a suggestion: "Why don't you explore the attic today? There are all kinds of interesting things up there in old trunks and boxes. Some of your folks' things too."

So up she goes, trailed as usual by Buster, now getting arthritic but still a loyal companion, and Laza, now in the prime of her life.

* * * * *

Late that evening, in her room, she lights her two kerosene lanterns and journals the story of a day that will always be with her:

Dear Anne,

Guess what I did today? Spent the day in the attic. It was drizzly out, so since Grandfather had a cold, he suggested I prowl around in the attic. What a day I've had!

First of all, I rummaged around in a box of my folks' things, not having any idea as to what I might find there. Near the bottom of the box I unearthed, in an empty Valentine's Day candy box, two big stacks of letters: one labeled "Robert," and one labeled "Jeannie." Her stack included many letters from Father during their friendship and then courtship days. His consisted only of letters she'd written him during that same time period. I decided to read hers to him first—and what a revelation that was! Some were written when she was only fourteen, and fifteen—my age. What a vivacious, delightful person she was! So excited about life, reading, music, and God. For the first time, I really felt I knew her! No

wonder she fascinated my father so. But then, later on, her letters turned tender. From then on I felt like an intruder, guilty because I was even reading them! One of them contained this line: "Robert, you wrote in your last letter that you love me. For so long had I considered you as just my best friend that your letter came as a bit of a jolt. But the more I thought about it, the more convicted I was that I've been for some time deeply in love with you—I just didn't know it!"

There were other letters written by my father to her that introduced me to a man I can barely remember. Made him three-dimensional to me. Made me, first, respect him; then, later, understand and love him. Then, I read his army letters to her. The one that really hit me was the very last one he ever wrote—to anyone! It was short:

Dearest Jeannie,

Darling, we're under heavy fire from the enemy, and frankly, it doesn't look good. Men are dying all around me. My best buddy was killed this afternoon. Now it is night, and I am writing this by flashlight. I'm addressing an envelope to you, I'll insert the letter when I'm done, seal it, then leave it at headquarters so it'll get to you even if I don't. I just wanted you to know—and precious Questa too, just in case she ever reads this: how very much I love you. You are what makes my life worth living. You are the first thing I think about when I awake and the last thing I think about at night! I thank God for you daily, that, unworthy of you as I am, you were willing to entrust your life to me.

And then there is Questa: the flesh-and-blood

evidence of our undying love for each other. If I don't make it, she will be the only lasting evidence I'll leave behind that only a great love could have made her possible. And God.

Oh, dearest one, shells are coming in. Looks like we'll have to fight it out tonight. If I don't ever get to see you in this world—thank God I'll see you in the kingdom!

Robert

The last lines were blurred from Mother's tears. I'm afraid I blurred them some more. The letter was mailed after his death.

Can't write any more—tell you the rest tomorrow.

Questa

A dream catcher

Dear Anne,

I've recovered—some. Don't think I'll ever be the same person I was before I read those letters. I'm afraid what was left of my childhood is now part of my past. I am a woman.

I did find some other treasures: some photos of my parents—both separate ones and together. Wedding photos too. The love light in their eyes—oh my!

Many other things I found, but these are the treasures I carried to my room and will cherish always!

One more thing: I found an exquisite rose-colored onyx jar in Grandmother's trunk. When I showed it to Grandfather, his face lit up: "My goodness! I forgot I still had that. I found it in an antique store, and it was hand-created by a Southwest Indian artist. You see, it even has a gold band attached to both the jar and the lid. It is called a dream catcher. The owner of it is supposed to insert into it only his or her most cherished dreams—and only that person should read them. I gave it to my bride just a few weeks before Robert was born, but she never had time to drop a dream into it. How fitting it is that you should be the one to find it. I am absolutely certain she'd have wanted you to have it so it can shelter your dreams. It's yours, dearest Questa."

So now, the dream catcher is on the shelf above my bed—waiting.

Questa

* * * * *

Two more years of the scroll of Questa's life unroll. They are quiet years: doing household chores, sewing, gardening with Uncle Hank, quilting with Aunt Ruth, working in the orchard with Grandfather, reading, walking the beach with Buster, going to church, once in a long while driving to town with Grandfather, writing in her journal, and every once in a while, dropping another dream into the dream catcher.

She sees no reason why this idyllic world should not go on forever.

But then . . .

Looking backward, looking forward

We can hear the thunder rattle and roar,
Can hear the tramp of the tide on the shore;

Hear the furious winds rush blustering by,
Or the pelting rain from a darkened sky.

We may hear the lark as he soaring sings,

Not the growth of the grass from whence he
   springs;

Nor hear we the soft snowflakes as they fall,
And trooping shroud the dead earth with a pall;

Nor yet the rise or descent of the dew,
That gems and freshens the rose and the rue;

Nor hear we the moments that make up time,
Though we tick them off with metallic chime;

Nor hear we the growth of the human soul,
Though demon or seraph may be the whole.

For thoughts and feelings come like the snow,
And virtues or vices like grass will grow;

And no moment slips to the silent sea
That makes not its mark for eternity.

—"Great Silences," by Mrs. G. Linnaeus Banks

Grandfather has gone on a business trip for an entire week, leaving Questa an assignment that appears easy but in reality is anything but. She's supposed to look back through the past nine years and then give *him* a grade for his teaching! She is to analyze—*dissect* is his preferred word—the teaching process that has brought her this far and critique it. In his words, "Don't be afraid to hurt my feelings: point out any failings that deserve to be pointed out, and don't praise me

unless you feel you absolutely have to. Both of us need to know what has worked best and what has fallen short so as we face the 'last stage,' we may know how to make appropriate course corrections."

Last stage, Questa thinks, that's scary! Grandfather has been my only teacher for so long that it terrifies me to think about how I can cope when I step out on my own for the very first time! I just hope it isn't coming very soon.

* * * * *

During this week of self-evaluation, Questa and Buster spend much of the time on the beach, exploring stretches far beyond where they've ever gone before. In her knapsack is a writing tablet, food for her and Buster, and other miscellaneous things. Every once in a while, when she finds an especially inviting spot by a sand dune or a large rock to protect them from the wind, she stops, takes out her tablet, and writes down thoughts that have come to her as she walked.

Finally, she forces herself to put it all into writing:

Let's see; how should I respond? Don't know how others teach, so I can't compare Grandfather to anyone else. That makes it hard. When I balked a bit, saying, "But Grandfather, I'm only fourteen! How can I know how to answer such questions?" he quietly responded with, "Do you realize that, on the American frontier, girls were expected to marry and start families when they were only fourteen, fifteen, and sixteen?" Goodness! Did that ever silence me! I'm certainly glad that's not true today!

So here goes: How does he teach? Well, he really doesn't; we learn together. When he brings up a subject, though he leads, I'm

expected to ask continual questions. He expects me to, in his words, "think," "reflect," "synthesize," to take no human being's thoughts or conclusions—including his—as valid until I weigh them in the balances of my own mind and decide on their merits myself. Until I test them through the "prism" (he likes that word) of God's eyes.

* * * * *

But that's not all he taught, I thought. How else would he want me to analyze his teaching?

Since I'm learning all the time, there's no structure that limits where the two of us go each day. So we go where excitement leads us. Consequently, it's never ever boring. Given that's true, I'm going to ramble now: He returns again and again to the sacredness of our time. He points out that in Christ's parables, no other subject gets as much emphasis as how we manage the time and talents He has entrusted to us. We seek serenity so that we can hear the "still small voice of God." He says, "You have it here, but when you leave this place, you'll find it in mighty short supply."

We explore nature together. We talk a lot about family, romance, and marriage, and why choosing the right mate is so crucial. "No decision you will ever make, Questa—other than whether or not to enter into daily partnership with God—is more serious than the choice of a life partner, for the wrong choice is likely to be catastrophic." We've talked much about the importance of family—other than God, the only bedrock we have. And we're never far from reveling in the spoken and written word—the beauty and power of using only the perfect words for our thoughts. He's big on memorization; that's why I've memorized thousands of pages of short stories and poems, including book-length poems such as Longfellow's "Evangeline" and "Hiawatha."

My oh my, does he ever emphasize reading, continual reading all through life! Also, he declares there is nothing in Scripture about retirement! Says that God expects us to continue growing as long as we live and breathe! His favorite age-related quote comes from The Youth's Instructor: "A life may be over at sixteen, or barely begun at seventy; it is the aim that determines its completeness." He's been warning me a lot lately about the intrusion of the technological world. Maintains that television has the potential to be the greatest time-waster ever devised.

History, to Grandfather, is not abstractions but biography . . . which is story. Christ never spoke without story—rarely in abstractions. Grandfather keeps emphasizing that we internalize values that are worth living only through the stories we love most, not through abstractions.

Says I should avoid cynicism and "poor me-ism." Beauty, unless it be inner beauty, is of little value. It's what's inside that counts.

Grandfather returns again and again to the subject of pride. He considers it to be the only "unpardonable sin." It's unpardonable not because God can't forgive it but because pride walls us off from God so that He can no longer communicate with us. Reason being: God will not invade our will!

As for foreign languages, he taught me Spanish so I could read Cervantes's Don Quixote in the original, and Greek so I could do the same with Homer's Iliad and Odyssey.

Grandfather and I are both excited about two British authors whose works we began reading J. R. R. Tolkien and C. S. Lewis. Grandfather considers the three little books Lewis published during World War II to be of particular value, especially the one devoted to the subject of what we permit to enter our minds. He warns that everything we experience, see, read, listen to, makes a "mark on the soul." When these marks come singly, we may feel that they're

not very important, but over time the marks tend to cluster, and the clusters grow into habits, and the habits grow into character, and character determines our eternal destiny. I've been thinking a lot about this subject and have concluded that I must not put anything into my mind that I don't want to live with for the rest of my life.

But of all the things Grandfather has talked to me about, nothing does he emphasize more than God's call to service for others. That selfless ministering to the Lord's sheep must be central in our life journey. That unless our love for God is translated into love for our fellow men, for all the other creatures that share our planet with us, then our abstract devotion to God is not only meaningless, it is a travesty. And parallel to this, Grandfather often returns to the subject of money: the more of it we have, the greater our responsibility to share with those most in need. He warns me that since a great deal of money is currently flowing in to us, it is imperative that we keep our lives simple, recognizing that none of it is our own to use selfishly.

* * * * *

So, how can I criticize nine years of all this? Whether or not he objects, when he comes back, I'm going to hug him half to death as I thank him—thank him for loving me enough to set my sails for life and eternity.

Fifteenth birthday

Because the road was steep and long
    And through a dark and lonely land,
God set upon my lips a song
    And put a lantern in my hand.

Through miles on weary miles of night
    That stretch relentless in my way,
My lantern burns serene and white,
    An unexhausted cup of day.

O golden lights and lights like wine
    How dim your boasted splendors are.
Behold this little lamp of mine;
    It is more starlike than a star!

—"Love's Lantern," by Joyce Kilmer

The storm-driven breakers are booming as they assault the rocky coast. Questa is drinking it all in from the recently constructed tea house out on a promontory that has long been her favorite dreaming spot. Knowing how much she loves it, Grandfather and Uncle Hank had surprised her by constructing it here—their gift to her on her fifteenth birthday.

She looks at her watch. Grandfather has promised to meet her here at sunset, a time of day both have always cherished. Early this morning, he said, "A blessed fifteenth birthday, my dear! You look radiant—and you're growing up." What he didn't say, but thought, was, *Oh my! You are the mirror image of your grandmother, just as beautiful as she ever was, and just as pure and unspoiled. You are the epitome of young womanhood. I am afraid—very afraid—of what certain young men will say and do in that great world out there, when I release you, give you freedom to soar.*

What he *did* say was, "I have something of extreme importance to share with you later today. Let's meet in the tea house just before sunset, and we'll talk."

Though Questa doesn't know what Grandfather will say, she has premonitions. Hints he's dropped in recent months. She doesn't know what, but senses that something is coming to an end, and something new is about to begin.

Before leaving her room, she picks up that most precious artifact, the dream catcher, and brings it with her. Then she sinks into the handmade chair he has created for her, the Dreaming Chair he calls it, and looks out at a sight she never tires of: the great Pacific . . . *How could I ever leave it!* she wonders.

After a time, she ever so gently opens the lid of the dream catcher and takes out, one at a time, the dreams she's dropped into it:

"I want to learn all there is to know." That one she'd written right after Grandfather had brought that ultimate Renaissance man, Leonardo da Vinci, to life for her.

"I want to be as faithful as my mother and father were to each other." That one she'd written shortly after finding the personal letters in the attic.

"I determine, with God's help, to remain humble always." She'd penned that after one of Grandfather's homilies on the dangers of pride.

"If it be God's will, may I find a man who'll love me as much as my mother and father, as my grandfather and grandmother, loved each other." That one she'd written the day after Grandfather shared with her the moving story of her grandmother's last moments.

"May I live each day to the hilt." Something about that metaphor intrigued her: that the shining sword of her existence would never be used as a plaything but instead it would be plunged into all life clear to the hilt—as far as it could go. Lines come to her now from Grandfather's favorite poem,

Tennyson's *Ulysses*, who, after fighting ten years at the city of Troy, roves the world for ten more long, adventurous years and then returns to his island kingdom of Ithaca—only to be bored with its sameness:

> I am a part of all that I have met;
> Yet all experience is an arch wherethrough
> Gleams that untraveled world, whose margin fades
> For ever and for ever when I move.
> How dull it is to pause, to make an end,
> To rust unburnished, not to shine in use!
> As though to breathe were life! Life piled on life
> Were all too little, and of one to me.
> Little remains; but every hour is saved
> From that eternal silence, something more,
> A bringer of new things; and vile it were
> For some three suns to store and hoard myself,
> And this grey spirit yearning in desire
> To follow knowledge like a sinking star,
> Beyond the utmost bound of human thought.

"May I be privileged to explore the world through travel." That one she'd written after memorizing a couple lines attributed to Saint Augustine: "The world is a great book, and those who never travel have read only one page."

"May I give each day my all, so that I may say to God, at the day's close, 'Lord, if You were to judge my entire life by what I've done this day, I would be content.' " She wrote this after Grandfather had her memorize "Salutation to the Dawn," penned fifteen hundred years ago by India's greatest poet, Kalidasa.

"May, if it be God's will, I be privileged to have children

of my own." That one she wrote one day after returning from leading out in one of the children's divisions in her church.

"May I always be blessed by books, books, and more books!" That one she'd written after another trip to the bookstore with Grandfather.

"May I be there for life, to take care of Grandfather as long as he lives." That one she wrote right after Grandfather's weeklong business trip.

"May I continue to conserve the forests and beauty spots for the American people." She determined to consider that family tradition a sacred trust.

"May I avoid putting anything in my memory bank I wouldn't want to live with for the rest of my life." She wrote that one after reading the little books that became C. S. Lewis's *Mere Christianity*.

"May ministering to the Lord's sheep remain my life's top priority." That was one of her most recent ones.

"May my life reflect the essence of Joyce Kilmer's poem 'Life's Lantern.' " She'd loved Kilmer's poetry ever since memorizing his poem "Trees."

* * * * *

Just as God gets out His paint brushes and begins to paint another sunset masterpiece in the west, Grandfather arrives, with Laza draped around his shoulders like a stole and Buster toiling behind him.

As the sun dips beyond the horizon, Grandfather says, "I told you I'd have something important to share with you. It is this: For ten long years now, you have given your studies your all, and I am ever so proud of all you've learned—and even

prouder of what you've *become*.

"But now, it is time I resist my yearning to keep you here by my side forever, and release you to other mentors. Enable you to interact with more people your own age. To move out from this ranch into the wider world.

"After much research, I have chosen a Christian boarding academy on the coast—a school that has a rigorous academic curriculum—as the place where you are to complete your high school years. I'll take you there, but I'll let you have the final say in the matter. You'll begin your junior year there next fall. It is my hope that your academy graduation will be followed by enrollment at a Christian college I've already checked into. You'll have the last say on that matter here too.

"I'm afraid that for a number of reasons you won't find this next step in your life an easy one to take. You are far more advanced academically than your fellow students are likely to be; and, in fact, even more advanced than some of your teachers. This won't make you very popular—especially among the boys, who are likely to view you as a threat grade-wise.

"And even among fellow Christians, you'll discover a herd mentality that will deeply disturb you. Also you'll see that it will be popular to be antireligious and to do and say things that will shock you. Yet if you seek out kindred spirits, you will always find them. You will make lasting friendships among those who share your Christ-centered philosophy of life.

"Socially, you're likely to be given the rush by boys. And you'll need all the character traits you've developed to hold out against temptations to do what is not right in God's eyes.

"You're likely to be disillusioned, but God will see you through. And I'll never be further away than a telephone call. When you need me, I'll come—no matter how far away

I may be. I'll pick you up for the longer breaks and summers. Next summer, you and I will begin the next stage of our explorations, and each summer we'll travel to places you've always wanted to see, both in this country and abroad.

"So now, dearest Questa, what are your thoughts?"

Her eighteenth Christmas

Questa is home from her first semester in college. Exhausted from final exams, she sleeps till noon the following day. Buster doesn't want to let her out of his sight; almost certainly he won't be alive next Christmas. Laza sulks whenever Questa dispossesses her of her lap.

When Grandfather asks her how things are going and if she likes the college, she responds with "Oh yes! It is so different from academy. They expect a lot more out of me now. And I have the sweetest roommate: her parents are missionaries in Latin America. She was taught

at home, too, so we have a lot in common."

"How about your teachers—what are they like?"

"Generally, I like them very much. But one of them fits one of your favorite quips very well: 'No one is ever completely useless. You can always serve as a horrible example.' My history professor is the other extreme. She's the first teacher I've had who reminds me of you. She's my advisor, so I know I'll be seeing a lot of her."

"And the spiritual dimension of campus life?"

"I'm so glad you warned me about that. I can always find both kinds, and I associate as much as possible with those who share my goals."

"Do you still journal?"

"You'll be glad to know that I continue to journal faithfully—usually, each day. And as you recommended, I work—in the cafeteria—twenty hours a week. The working students are, by and large, those I admire most."

Tell me your dream

How as a child I used to tease,

"Tell me your dream—I will tell you mine, too!"
They told me whatever they thought would please,
 And I waited to see the omen come true.
 My childhood fancy I still pursue,
Though in other wise, and on each I call
"Tell me your dream!" . . . But your dream is *you*.
We are our dreams—and the Dream is all.

Do not deride me, do not deny,
 And point me not to the things you have *done*,
But tell me your dream! Have you held thereby—
 The clue that was with your destiny spun,
 Walked with it ever, through shadow and sun?
Does the vision remain?—no ill shall befall;
 Lost? —there is nothing worthwhile to be won!
We are our dreams—and the Dream is all.

Oh, why to memorial places repair,
 Where the lamps in the shrines perpetually burn?
Your hero, your saint, or your sage is not *there*:
 Born of his dream, his deeds can but earn
 That unto a dream in the end they return!
For this, is the trophy, the wreath, on the wall;
 And for this is your worship, that well ye may learn
We are our dreams—and the Dream is all.

—"Tell Me Your Dream," by Edith M. Thomas

Grandfather is tired, so Questa retires early. Climbs up the stairs to her beloved fourth-floor tower room. How dear it is! But different—because it is no longer a child's room, but rather a young woman's. Yet, the things she loves most are still here.

Even though it is cold outside, as always the door to the veranda is ajar just enough so she can listen to the heavenly sound of the waves rolling in, in the sea's eternal tryst with the shore. There's a fire burning in her fireplace, Laza is curled up next to her, and Buster is close by on the rug. He's too old and arthritic to jump up on the bed anymore.

On this moonlit December night in the year of our Lord, 1954, she gives her thoughts free rein to roam:

Dear, dear Grandfather—for the first time ever, I noticed his frailty. Always before, he's seemed indestructible. How much longer I'll have him I have no idea. All I know is that I must cherish each moment I have left with him.

So very many memories are tied to this place. When Mother brought me here—has it really been twelve long years ago?—I was shy, scared, insecure, and desperately unhappy. Here in this heavenly place, Grandfather has given me wings . . . has sheltered my dreams.

So, quo vadis, Questa? I really don't know. I have no idea where my dreams will take me. Only God can know that. What I do know is that I can trust His leading.

It's rather strange: some of my college teachers appear to be a little in awe of my mind. Same for my classmates. Grandfather was right: a number of the boys view me as a threat where grades are concerned. Most of the coeds have no career dreams outside of marriage; consequently, they don't know what to think of me when I tell them I want both. Many envy me my opportunities to travel; their worlds are so small and confined compared to mine.

Date-wise, Grandfather was right there too: The boys have given me the proverbial "rush," but I have not yet found any whom

I conceivably might someday consider to be the one. I'm actually glad that's so, because I've just begun to test my wings for longer flights.

But I do know that the dream catcher must remain with me—and one by one I shall continue to drop in each dream as it comes.

* * * * *

The beautifully decorated tree has grudgingly surrendered its presents. The fire is crackling in the fireplace. Candles and kerosene lanterns remind Questa of old times.

After the presents have been unwrapped and exclaimed over, all four settle back into their cushions and let their minds wander through this wondrous night and times past. Grandfather can't keep his eyes off Questa. The firelight brings iridescence to her long, raven hair. *She's everything I hoped she'd be: a lovely young woman inside and out; one who loves the good Lord. How devastated I would be if she had lost her way in that dangerous world out there.*

Questa breaks the reverie. "Grandfather, what story are you reading to us tonight? Your annual Christmas story is something I look forward to every year. I hope you've saved an especially good one for us."

Grandfather answers, "The very best! For years I've been saving it for this *very* special occasion."

"Special? How different from our other Christmases, Grandfather?"

"Special because it's your eighteenth Christmas. The bridge between your youth and your adulthood. For this long-awaited occasion I've saved perhaps the greatest Christmas story ever written outside of Holy Writ: Henry Van Dyke's

The Other Wise Man. I saved it, Questa, because in its pages you will find everything I have tried to instill in you during all your growing-up years. It is a story I hope you will return to, in one way or another, every other Christmas of your life. By the time I finish reading it, you will know why I make such a request.

"Van Dyke was convicted that the story was God's, not his, for it came to him in all its fullness one night in a dream. Like you, Questa, Artaban had his own dreams—and he did his utmost to make them come true. But God had dreams for Artaban too—and you will see, in the story, who won out."

Grandfather now opens the book, puts on his spectacles, and begins reading, "In the days when August Caesar was master of many kings and Herod reigned in Jerusalem, there lived in . . ."

Grandfather's sonorous voice then carries the story to its moving conclusion almost an hour later: Twice, Artaban, the fourth wise man, had used one of the three gems intended for the King to save individuals for whom he was their last hope. And now, as he approached Jerusalem's Damascus gate not far from a hill called Golgotha,

a troop of Macedonian soldiers came down the street, dragging a young girl with torn dress and disheveled hair. As the Magian paused to look at her with compassion, she broke suddenly from the hands of her tormentors and threw herself at his feet, clasping him around the knees. She had seen his white cap and the winged circle on his breast.

"Have pity on me," she cried, "and save me, for the sake of the God of Purity! I also am a daughter

of the true religion which is taught by the Magi. My father was a merchant of Parthia, but he is dead, and I am seized for his debts to be sold as a slave. Save me from worse than death!"

Artaban trembled.

It was the old conflict in his soul, which had come to him in the palm-grove of Babylon and in the cottage at Bethlehem—the conflict between the expectation of faith and the impulse of love. Twice the gift which he had consecrated to the worship of religion had been drawn from his hand to the service of humanity. This was the third trial, the ultimate probation, the final and irrevocable choice.

Was it his great opportunity or his last temptation? He could not tell. One thing only was clear in the darkness of his mind—it was inevitable. And does not the inevitable come from God?

One thing only was sure to his divided heart—to rescue this helpless girl would be a true deed of love. And is not love the light of the soul?

He took the pearl from his bosom. Never had it seemed so luminous, so radiant, so full of tender, living luster. He laid it in the hand of the slave.

"This is thy ransom, daughter! It is the last of my treasures which I kept for the King."

While he spoke, the darkness of the sky thickened, and shuddering tremors ran through the earth, heaving convulsively like the breast of one who struggles with mighty grief.

The walls of the houses rocked to and fro. Stones were loosened and crashed into the street.

Dust clouds filled the air. The soldiers fled in terror, reeling like drunken men. But Artaban and the girl whom he had ransomed crouched helpless beneath the wall of the Prætorium.

What had he to fear? What had he to live for? He had given away the last remnant of his tribute for the King. He had parted with the last hope of finding Him. The quest was over, and it had failed. But, even in that thought, accepted and embraced, there was peace. It was not resignation. It was not submission. It was something more profound and searching. He knew that all was well, because he had done the best that he could, from day to day. He had been true to the light that had been given to him. He had looked for more. And if he had not found it, if a failure was all that came out of his life, doubtless that was the best that was possible. He had not seen the revelation of "life everlasting, incorruptible, and immortal." But he knew that even if he could live his earthly life over again, it could not be otherwise than it had been.

One more lingering pulsation of the earthquake quivered through the ground. A heavy tile, shaken from the roof, fell and struck the old man on the temple. He lay breathless and pale, with his gray head resting on the young girl's shoulder, and the blood trickling from the wound. As she bent over him, fearing that he was dead, there came a voice through the twilight, very small and still, like music sounding from a distance, in which the notes are clear but the words are lost. The girl turned to see if

someone had spoken from the window above them, but she saw no one.

Then the old man's lips began to move, as if in answer, and she heard him say in the Parthian tongue:

"Not so, my Lord: For when saw I thee an-hungered, and fed thee? Or thirsty, and gave thee drink? When saw I thee a stranger, and took thee in? Or naked, and clothed thee? When saw I thee sick or in prison, and came unto thee? Three-and-thirty years have I looked for thee; but I have never seen thy face, nor ministered to thee, my King."

He ceased, and the sweet voice came again.

And again the maid heard it, very faintly and far away. But now it seemed as though she understood the words:

"Verily I say unto thee, inasmuch as thou hast done it unto one of the least of these my brethren, thou hast done it unto me."

A calm radiance of wonder and joy lighted the pale face of Artaban like the first ray of dawn on a snowy mountain-peak. One long, last breath of relief exhaled gently from his lips.

His journey was ended. His treasures were accepted. The Other Wise Man had found the King.

How this story came to be

For an entire year I wrestled with God, asking Him, if it be His will, that He would entrust me with a story of His choosing, a story that would be His rather than mine, a story that would bless all who read it or heard it. But month after month went by. In the interim, I tried several leads, but none of them jelled.

Finally, I wrestled like Jacob with God for the story—and it came at last, but only the setting and the lead characters. I set them loose and followed them for thirty pages of handwritten text. Then the story got away from me. In desperation I prayed again, and this time I was impressed to leave the northern Rocky Mountain setting, move it to the Northwest Pacific Coast—and start all over again.

This time I was impressed to make Questa's story a mirror image of my own life-journey, even to the day, month, and year of her birth. Those years, of course, I knew inside out, having experienced each moment of them. But at that point, I gave the lead characters back to God, leaving the day-to-day evolution of the plot in His hands. Never, from one day to the next, did I have any idea as to how the story would move on or conclude. Not until the very last day of the story's writing did I know for sure how it would end.

But naturally, if the story were to have power, it must ring true as I drew from experiences and influences in my own life: I was personally homeschooled (before there was even a term for it) for fourteen of the first sixteen years of my life by my missionary/teacher mother, Barbara Leininger Wheeler, in the then remote world of Latin America. Mother was a talented elocutionist with a near photographic memory. She had memorized thousands of pages of short stories and poetry, including book-length poems such as Longfellow's "Hiawatha" and "Evangeline."

Mother it was who unleashed me on library after library and encouraged me to check out and read whatever interested me most. Even though she was a conservative Christian, she placed no limitations on what I read, trusting me to make the right choices. Mother was my pied piper to all that the great world had to offer. She was the same for my brother, Romayne, who went on to earn two doctorates in music in Vienna, Austria, and is today a renowned concert pianist who performs all around the world. And also for my sister, Marjorie, who is today an award-winning artist with the brush and an art teacher. My father, on the other hand, was the spiritual rock of our home. My parents were passionately in love with each other, and remained so until the very end.

Then stir in my one-of-a-kind maternal grandfather, Herbert Norton Leininger, a true Renaissance man who earned his living as a florist. I was privileged to live with him and Grandmother Josephine for my eighth-grade year. Grandfather loved drama and poetry and could quote it by the hour. He also knew Shakespeare's Hamlet by heart. His house walls were papered with National Geographic maps, and he seemed to know everything that was going on in the world and exactly where on the maps it was taking place.

Other than my mother, the most significant contributor to the persona of Grandfather in the story was Dr. Walter Utt, chairman of the history department at Pacific Union College in California's Napa Valley. Dr. Utt was, without question, the central mentor of my life. I worked for him for three years, one as his graduate assistant, and I took every course, undergraduate and graduate, that he taught. He had the God-given

ability to turn abstract lecture notes into story—stories so real that it seemed the people in them were right there in our classroom. We'd lose all track of time until the bell rang and we re-entered that other world. And there was no expiration date to Dr. Utt's mentoring: he was there for us through life.

The California, Oregon, and Washington coasts are mine by inheritance. I can remember living without electricity, plumbing, or telephones and bathing in copper tubs with fireplace- or stove-heated water, and outdoor privies too. Roads were more often than not unpaved. Girls and women were stereotyped and limited to such occupations as teaching and nursing. All women were expected to marry and sublimate their career dreams to their husbands' (which was true of my parents' generation, and partly true of mine). Buster, my paternal grandfather's dog, weighed 120 pounds. When I returned after a three-year absence, he was so deliriously excited to see me that he jumped up and clicked teeth with me. I lost two of my central ones as a result. At that time, people lived a simpler and far more serene life than do today's children. Thus they were given silence in which to dream and to become.

The story also incorporates a parallel to my own leaving home and traveling alone to an academy on the California coast when I was only sixteen. Because my missionary parents lived so far away, I never lived at home again; I just went there to visit. Questa is luckier than I in that respect. Like

Questa, I too was, and still am, a dreamer. It is extremely unlikely that I'll ever again write a story that draws as much from my own journey as does this one—even to the Pearl Harbor section. Even though at the time I was only five on December 7, 1941, I can still remember Dad coming home in the middle of the day, making that terrible announcement, and turning on the radio.

* * *

Today, homeschooling is sweeping the nation. And because of the breakdown of the home—which has resulted in the devaluation of marriage and lifetime commitment and in skyrocketing divorce rates and live-in relationships becoming the new norm—and because of the inability of so many single mothers to cope, one-third of all children today are, in effect, being raised by their grandparents.

God impressed me to address all these factors, at least by contrast, in the pages of this story.

And finally, the story would have been much less were it not for the fact that it had to run through the gauntlet of four eagle-eyed, pro-bono editor/readers: Linda Steinke of Alberta, Sheree Nudd of Maryland, Greg Wheeler of Florida, and Ellen Francisco of Tennessee.

Bless them!

Sources

In the order in which they appeared in the story.

Finley, C. F. "The Midnight Limited." *Munsey's Magazine,* January 1906. Original text owned by Joe Wheeler.

Morris, Gouverneur. "To a Little Child." *The Century Magazine,* December 1904. Original text owned by Joe Wheeler.

Paine, Albert Bigelow. "Sand Houses." *Munsey's Magazine,* June 1898. Original text owned by Joe Wheeler.

Stidger, William L. "The Child and the Book." In *Anthology of the World's Best Poems, Vol. II.* Selected by Edwin Markham. New York: William H. Wise & Co., 1948. Text owned by Joe Wheeler.

Dickinson, Emily. "Your Thoughts Don't Have Words Every Day." In *The Complete Poems of Emily Dickinson.* Edited by Thomas H. Johnson. Boston: Little, Brown & Co., 1960. If anyone knows the first publication source and date, please send to Joe Wheeler (P.O. Box 1246, Conifer, CO 80433).

Upton, Melville. "Absence." *The Century Magazine,* June 1896. Original text owned by Joe Wheeler.

Banks, Mrs. G. Linnaeus. "Great Silences." *The Girl's Own Paper,* October 5, 1899. Original text owned by Joe Wheeler.

Kilmer, Joyce. "Love's Lantern." *The Century Magazine,* March 1914. Original text owned by Joe Wheeler.

Tennyson, Alfred, Lord. "Ulysses." In *The Complete Works of Alfred Tennyson.* New York: Hurst & Co., n.d. Original text owned by Joe Wheeler.

Thomas, Edith M. "Tell Me Your Dream." *Harper's Monthly Magazine,* January 1921. Original text owned by Joe Wheeler.

Van Dyke, Henry. *The Other Wise Man.* New York: Harper Brothers Publishers, 1920. Original text owned by Joe Wheeler.

Celebrate Christmas with these classic stories!

Read a story from Joe L. Wheeler's
CHRISTMAS IN MY HEART series every night in December—
there are plenty of stories to choose from:

CHRISTMAS IN MY HEART 17
Paperback, 128 Pages
ISBN 13: 978-0-8163-2286-2

CHRISTMAS IN MY HEART 18
Paperback, 128 Pages
ISBN 13: 978-0-8163-2360-9

CHRISTMAS IN MY HEART 19
Paperback, 128 Pages
ISBN 13: 978-0-8163-2406-4

CHRISTMAS IN MY HEART 20
Paperback, 128 Pages
ISBN 13: 978-0-8163-2476-7

CHRISTMAS IN MY HEART 21
Paperback, 128 Pages
ISBN 13: 978-0-8163-3401-8

CHRISTMAS IN MY HEART 22
Paperback, 128 Pages
ISBN 13: 978-0-8163-4436-9

CHRISTMAS IN MY HEART 23
Paperback, 128 Pages
ISBN 13: 978-0-8163-5422-1

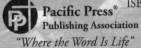
Pacific Press®
Publishing Association
"Where the Word Is Life"

AdventistBookCenter.com   f AdventistBookCenter   🐦 @AdventistBooks   YouTube AdventistBooks

Three ways to order:

1 Local	Adventist Book Center®	
2 Call	1-800-765-6955	
3 Shop	AdventistBookCenter.com	